THE FORTUNES OF TEXAS

Follow the lives and loves of a complex family with a rich history and deep ties in the Lone Star State

FORTUNE'S HIDDEN TREASURES

A new branch of the Fortune family heads to idyllic Emerald Ridge to solve a decades-long mystery that died with their parents, and a mysterious loss that upends their lives. Little do they know that their hearts will never be the same!

FORTUNE ON HIS DOORSTEP

The irresistible woman with a magnetic hold on his triplets might just be the answer to all of tycoon Trevor Porter's problems. And it's a fair trade—when the widower and his brood move into a home adjacent to the Fortune family compound during their nanny search, Kelsey Fortune's ranch-running woes might be a thing of her past! But can off-the-charts attraction pave the way to playing house... for real?

Dear Reader,

It was a pleasure writing *Fortune on His Doorstep*. This is my second time participating in the Fortunes of Texas continuity and my first time penning a story featuring triplets.

Kelsey and Trevor shared one of my favorite meet-cutes ever and that was all because of the triplets. Those adorable Porters are hard to resist but fun to write. Though Kelsey felt some trepidation about dating a man with children, she decided to trust her intuition. And with Kelsey's encouragement, Trevor was able to let go of his past hurt in order to embrace a much happier future.

My favorite thing about Kelsey and Trevor was how wild their chemistry was. The intensity between them was more than assuaging a physical need. They also bonded over their love for the children as well as shared hobbies and interests. I enjoyed seeing their relationship expand from attraction to friendship then to love.

I really hope you enjoy reading these characters' journey to love as much as I did. I would love to hear from you. Please consider joining my mailing list at michellelindorice.com.

Best,

Michelle

FORTUNE
ON HIS DOORSTEP

MICHELLE LINDO-RICE

Harlequin

THE FORTUNES OF TEXAS

If you purchased this book without a cover you should be aware that this book is stolen property. It was reported as "unsold and destroyed" to the publisher, and neither the author nor the publisher has received any payment for this "stripped book."

Special thanks and acknowledgment are given to
Michelle Lindo-Rice for her contribution to
The Fortunes of Texas: Fortune's Hidden Treasures miniseries.

Harlequin®
THE FORTUNES OF TEXAS

Recycling programs for this product may not exist in your area.

ISBN-13: 978-1-335-14328-0

Fortune on His Doorstep

Copyright © 2025 by Harlequin Enterprises ULC

All rights reserved. No part of this book may be used or reproduced in any manner whatsoever without written permission.

Without limiting the author's and publisher's exclusive rights, any unauthorized use of this publication to train generative artificial intelligence (AI) technologies is expressly prohibited.

This is a work of fiction. Names, characters, places and incidents are either the product of the author's imagination or are used fictitiously. Any resemblance to actual persons, living or dead, businesses, companies, events or locales is entirely coincidental.

For questions and comments about the quality of this book, please contact us at CustomerService@Harlequin.com.

TM and ® are trademarks of Harlequin Enterprises ULC.

Harlequin Enterprises ULC
22 Adelaide St. West, 41st Floor
Toronto, Ontario M5H 4E3, Canada
www.Harlequin.com

MIX
Paper | Supporting responsible forestry
FSC® C021394

Printed in Lithuania

Michelle Lindo-Rice is the author of *The Bookshop Sisterhood*, an Emma Award winner and an RWA Vivian Award finalist. Michelle enjoys reading and crafting fiction across genres. Originally from Jamaica, West Indies, she has earned degrees from New York University; SUNY at Stony Brook; Teachers College, Columbia University; and Argosy University and has been an educator for over twenty years. She also writes as Zoey Marie Jackson.

Books by Michelle Lindo-Rice

The Fortunes of Texas: Fortune's Hidden Treasures

Fortune on His Doorstep

The Fortunes of Texas: Fortune's Secret Children

A Fortune Thanksgiving

Harlequin Special Edition

The Valentine's Do-Over
A Beauty in the Beast

Seven Brides for Seven Brothers

Rivals at Love Creek
Cinderella's Last Stand
Twenty-Eight Dates
An Alaskan Arrangement

Visit the Author Profile page
at Harlequin.com for more titles.

For my husband, John, and my sons, Eric and Jordan.

Thank you to my assistant, Sobi, and my agent, Latoya Smith, as well as Susan, Katixa, Gail and all the members of the Harlequin team.

And a special thanks for my faithful readers and book clubs who continue to support all my writing endeavors.

Chapter One

It had only been eighteen hours, twelve minutes and nine seconds since his father had left for his month-long cruise with his fiancée, Manuela. Yep, Trevor Porter was already on a countdown, desperate for his pop's return.

Standing in the kitchen of the gorgeous mansion he had rented while his new house was finished being built in Emerald Ridge, Trevor tried to focus on the calm of the river visible through the huge bay windows instead of the cacophony caused by his nine-month-old triplets wriggling about in their high chairs. Remembering his father's advice that Trevor should get back into the dating world, he snorted. As if any woman would willingly want the responsibility of dating a man with three kids.

Just getting them all dressed and strapped in for breakfast had been a task. Since Halloween had been the day before and he had purchased two outfits, Trevor had decided to dress them in outfit number two today. Yesterday they had worn bee rompers with matching caps while he had been their beekeeper. Today they wore pumpkin outfits, but he'd had to change his Dad of the Patch coordinated T-shirt.

Note to self: Don't get dressed before giving the kids

a bath. And don't forget to put on their bibs before feeding them.

Within seconds of tucking them into their high chairs, most of their cheerios and scrambled eggs had been scattered on the kitchen floor.

He ran a hand over his beard and groaned. There was no way he was going to be able to care for the triplets on his own for the next twenty-eight days. An extra pair of hands made all the difference in the world when you had hungry mouths to feed. Tending to them was so much easier when Pop was around. He treasured having family around.

It was actually because of newfound family—cousins, Imani and Jonathan—that Trevor had even ventured to Emerald Ridge. He had such a sense of belonging with both his cousins and the land that Trevor had decided to raise his family here.

Sighing, he rubbed between his eyes as his words to his father came back to him. *Don't worry, Pop, enjoy the Caribbean seas, I've got this.*

If those words could be eaten, his thirty-one-year-old tummy would be full. Because the only thing he had was three squirming, crying babies.

That's why Trevor had placed an ad for a temporary live-in within an hour of his father's departure in the town's online community social page. He eyed the clock. He had already interviewed two applicants and neither seemed capable of handling one, much less three babies. His final candidate was due any minute. Hopefully, he would get his children settled before she arrived.

Sasha let out a bellow loud enough to rattle the glassware in the china cabinet. Covering his ears, Trevor reached over to pluck William's foot out of his mouth before settling his son back into his high chair. He ducked his head, narrowly missing the fistful of scrambled eggs James threw his way. The eggs landed on his T-shirt that his late wife, Claudia, had purchased when they learned they were going to be parents of three and not one baby. This was the first time he had actually donned it, and he had to scoff at the words. Being a Dad of Triplets Means Having Three Times the Fun.

He had chosen it to boost his spirits, but the words now only served as a beacon to remind him what a woeful job he was doing since his wife's passing. He was surviving minute by minute—no, make that *second by second*. Trevor jumped and yelped as something cold and wet hit his cheeks. That move made Sasha stop mid-cry before her body shook with laughter. He brushed the eggs off because he wasn't changing a third time.

"Oh, you think it's funny that Daddy has egg face," he said, wiping his face and then playing with her cheeks. Sasha dissolved into laughter even more. Trevor looked into the little face, which resembled her mom, and his heart pinched. Sasha had taken her first step yesterday, and he had managed to capture the moment on camera. He had cheered so loud that he had startled his baby girl and she'd fallen to her bum before her chin wobbled with tears.

Gosh, he wished Claudia had lived to see their children's milestones. But a mere week after childbirth, she had passed suddenly from a weakened heart muscle, and he had found himself a single dad of three. He had needed family. That's why Trevor had taken time off from his beef cattle business, Porter Cuts, an hour away in Dallas. He was fortunate to have the staff and capital so he could wait until the triplets were a year old before returning to work. That was his game plan.

"Dadadadada," James said, pumping his feet hard enough to move the high chair.

Trevor patted his head and scooped up some eggs out of the blue plastic bowl to give to his son. He gave William a quick glance and sighed. His son's foot was back in his mouth again, his sock discarded somewhere. It was always the left foot and always the big toe.

"I bet all that toe needs is some ketchup," he joked. Trevor looked around for the errant footwear, finding it underneath Sasha's leg. After he put it on, he stepped back and decided to take a picture of his children. With her light brown eyes, olive-toned skin and curly hair, Sasha was already Claudia's mini-me. William, however, was all Trevor and his mom, Samira, with skin the color of smooth brown sand, twinkling dark brown eyes and a ready smile. While James was a blend of the both of them, with Claudia's deep dimples and complexion and his height. All three faces and clothes were covered with eggs and milk from their sippy cups.

Seeing those chins tilted up at him with such trust made his eyes well. Claudia had been so right when she had said there was more to life than work. His wife's mantra had been ingrained in him. But he had been too stubborn to listen, too focused on accumulating his wealth, on making Porter Cuts thrive. Yes, they had had their problems—he had been a workaholic—but Trevor would trade all his success to have her back with him, to give his children a mother.

He knew what it was like, having lost his own mother when he was eighteen years old. He walked around feeling like his heart was permanently cinched with crab's claws. And days like today, it squeezed harder than others.

His cell phone rang. It was Jonathan calling. He answered the phone and put on *Timmy & Friends* on YouTube to entertain the children while they ate.

"How's the nanny situation going?" his cousin asked. The fact that he *had* a cousin made Trevor's chest expand. Growing up an only child with a single mom, he'd felt pretty lonely at times, but it wasn't until Samira was on her deathbed that she had confessed to him his true heritage. That he was the grandson of tycoon Hammond Porter, a fact he resented. The discovery of blood relatives near his age had been the only reward so far.

"It's going," Trevor heaved out. "I have one more today, and if that doesn't work out, I don't know what I'm going to do." A splat of something hit his back. Something squishy and wet. Reaching a hand behind him, he brushed away the egg.

"Just offer a larger bonus," Jonathan suggested.

"Great idea." The doorbell rang. Of course, the triplets broke into a wail. His cousin was saying something and Trevor had to press the phone closer to his ear.

"Whoa. It sounds like you have your hands full. Do you need me to drop over?"

"I might have to take you up on that offer, but I hope to be hiring someone today."

"Oh, good. Well, keep me posted."

Praying the person on the other side of the door would be *the one*, Trevor scurried out the kitchen, past the family room littered with laundry and filled with scattered toys, then swung open the front door. Even though the triplets were secure, the cries behind him had escalated, putting him on edge. There was an older woman standing at the door with her arms crossed who introduced herself as Ms. Quinn. Though it was a beautiful autumn day, she wore a lined business suit, and even with the light breeze, her bun was firmly in place. He invited her inside, hiding his smirk at her pursed lips once she had taken in the state of his home.

"I have a housekeeper," he felt compelled to offer. "It didn't look like this yesterday and it won't look like this at the end of the day."

Ms. Quinn poked her nose in the air and sniffed. "The key is to clean as you go," she said, her tone disapproving. "Your children will need order. Structure." She scanned the area, frowning at the dollop of sweet potatoes on the edge of the coffee table—or at least he hoped that was what that was—and shook her head. "This is chaos." Right on cue, his children's cry level boosted. Ms. Quinn covered her ears and shook her head. "Unacceptable. I can see they will need to be kept in line."

Her stiff tone made his hackles rise. He wanted a doting, loving nanny, not a drill sergeant. Trevor swallowed his irritation and pointed to the front door. "I don't think we need to continue," he said, jogging toward the kitchen. "I've got to go tend to my children." He gestured to the front door. "I trust you can see your way out."

"But you didn't ask any questions," she sputtered from behind him.

"Don't need to. You've already shown me enough of who you are," he tossed over his shoulder, dismissing her from his mind. A second later, he heard the door slam and satisfaction filled his chest. Good riddance. Boy, he wished he could have someone like Jonathan's son's caretaker, but his cousin wasn't about to share his nanny with anyone.

Trevor rushed to the nursery and retrieved a box of wipes. James's and Sasha's faces were red from crying. Will just sat checking out his siblings, though his eyes welled. The minute they saw him, their cries ceased, their little chins wobbling. "It's alright. It's alright," he cooed. "Daddy's here."

Releasing James and William first, Trevor wiped their faces and hands. He placed them into the large playpen in the family room. Then he retrieved Sasha and did the same. Just before he put her with her brothers, Trevor got a whiff that told him that she needed changing. He slapped his forehead.

Diapers.

Pop had told him at least three times to order diapers. With three babies in the house, Trevor used a mail-order service, but Orson had stated there was a glitch, so the order hadn't processed. That had been two days ago.

He dashed into the children's nursery with Sasha wriggling in his arms—a converted master bedroom—and counted the stack. He was down to twenty-seven. That might be enough until morning. But, then again it might not. Grabbing three and a box of wipes, Trevor placed Sasha on the changing table. She was squirming so much, he ended up ripping the tab off the diaper. And then another.

At this rate he would be out of diapers before dinner. He was going to have to head out to the store. And he might as well stop at the farmers market to get some fresh fruit and veggies to puree for the kids' food. Making their own baby food was something Claudia had wanted to do for the children, and so far, he had kept up with that.

Quickly finishing up with Sasha, he cleaned James and Will then packed the trio into their car seats. Since he drove a large SUV, Trevor was able to fit a wagon in the third row and the stroller in the trunk. After grabbing a fully stocked diaper bag, Trevor packed the triplets into his rear seat and drove over to the general store. It wasn't until he was about to head to the farmers market that he considered he might not have any room for his farm haul. He rested against the doorjamb of the passenger seat and released a long breath. He felt like he had run a marathon instead of shopping for necessities.

Maybe he should head home and do this another day.

No can do. Stopping at home would mean he would be bumping close to nap time. He would pick out his goods and then see if the farm offered delivery. With that plan in mind, Trevor grabbed the stroller wagon and strapped his children inside before tugging them down the gravelly path. He figured they would find it fun while he shopped, but he was oh so wrong. Because all he saw were panicked faces and hands gripping the sides of the wagon as their bodies heaved forward and backward.

Suddenly his morning had gone from bad to worse.

* * *

Kelsey Fortune loved this time of year—the foliage of reds, yellows, oranges and greens, the crunching leaves under her feet. The weather was chef's kiss perfect, and she welcomed the smells of autumn. If it weren't for the fact that her newly purchased ranch, Fortune 8, could be in trouble, this would count as one of her best days ever.

All Kelsey wanted was for her ranch to flourish. But taking care of her cattle, sheep and horses was too much to do alone, especially now that she had rashly fired her foreman and workers. Her pair of old jeans, a white tee and a flannel shirt, along with her boots and cowgirl hat, were the practical choice for the grueling labor she'd had to do at the crack of dawn before driving to the Emerald Ridge Farmers Market to buy supplies. A tedious task made bearable because she was meeting up with her cousin to shop together and engage in some small talk since Kelsey hadn't had time to socialize the past month.

Priscilla was already there when she arrived. Kelsey pulled up next to her. The cousins squealed and shared a hug like they hadn't seen each other in years.

When Priscilla's parents, Mark and Marlene, died in a plane crash two decades earlier, Kelsey had been just three years old, and her father had only been twenty-four. But, despite being young and grieving, her dad moved with Kelsey into the Fortune mansion to take care of Priscilla and her siblings, Roth, Harris and Zara. At twenty-eight, Priscilla was the nearest to Kelsey in age, which was why they were so close.

"It feels like forever since I've seen you," Priscilla said. "I was so glad when you reached out for us to meet up."

"I know. It's been a minute since we've hung out. The ranch takes up so much of my time. That's why I started the family group chat so I can keep us all in the loop."

Arm in arm, the cousins walked together from the parking lot up the path toward the market, enjoying the brilliant blue skies on this fine November day. There were a lot of other shoppers milling about, including parents with their little ones. This was one of the must-go places in town. In addition to being a market, there were farm rides and a small café. She could smell the apple cinnamon donuts and roasted pecans, which she would make sure to get before leaving.

To the right of the shop, there was a pumpkin stand with a gaggle of children carving away on some of the benches. She grinned at the kids' joyful squeals. If she weren't pressed for time, she would definitely join them.

Kelsey grabbed a flatbed while Priscilla reached for a cart, and they went into the main store. She then filled her flatbed with oversize bags of apples and carrots for her horses and a bushel of corn for her cows. Kelsey didn't relish having to hoist her feed in her truck bed later. But she decided to let later worry about itself.

Kelsey and Priscilla made sure to avoid the piles of pumpkin slosh as they made their way to the vegetables.

"How is it going with your foreman?" Priscilla asked.

"Oh, don't get me started." She had inherited Young with the property, and every time she spoke to him, he smirked, calling her *Little Lady*, which encouraged the ranch hands and cowboys to do the same.

"But that's not even the worse of it. I learned that Young has been making fun of me on social media. He has quite a following commenting and laughing at everything I do. I know I'm only twenty-five," she grumbled, "but I'm still very much their boss and I deserve their respect."

"Ugh, that man is just beyond insulting," her cousin said, putting some celery into her handheld basket. "I doubt he would do this if you were a man."

"I agree. Young used every opportunity to undermine my authority, and that grew old really fast."

"You know he's salty because you won the bid over his uncle for the ranch."

She waved at a little girl eating an ice cream cone though it was only half past ten. "Yup. I can't believe I fell for his lies. Young had given me some sob story about being a single dad and having to take care of his teen daughter. Something he made up so he could record my response and post for likes. Can you believe that?"

"This guy sounds like a real jerk."

"He is. And he's free to join his uncle over at his ranch. I let him go this morning."

Priscilla nodded. "It sounds like you made a great decision. Who did you hire as his replacement?"

"Um… I'm going to put up some ads this morning." She pointed to the small stack of signs, nails and hammer in her purse. "I've already posted a few."

Her cousin frowned and gently squeezed her arm. "Kelsey, I know this guy has been awful and I sympathize with you, but you shouldn't have fired Young until you secured another foreman."

Tilting her head back, she met Priscilla's hazel ones. "Actually, I fired all of my workers."

Priscilla's mouth dropped. She tucked her blond tendrils away behind her ear. "All of them? So, you've been running the ranch by yourself? Please tell me you haven't been doing all those ranch chores all alone."

"Yes, two days ago, and I'll honor your wishes by not telling you I've been handling feed, mucking stalls and checking for lice on my own for a couple of days." She walked toward the register, putting all her strength into pushing the flatbed. Her cousin caught up to her and they joined the queue. "Now, before you chide me for being too hasty, I have zero regrets." She squared her shoulders. "Correction. I had no regrets until I remembered that my starter herds are set to be delivered by the end of this week and it's almost lambing time for a couple of my ewes." She shuddered at the thought of managing a cattle herd of forty and birthings by herself.

"Th-this week?" Priscilla sputtered, her eyes wide. "You're being way too calm for my liking. You need to hire help pronto."

Kelsey blew out a breath. "I wish I could hire an all-female crew."

"That would be hard to pull off in a town as small as Emerald Ridge." They stepped closer to the register.

"A girl can dream, can't she?" she muttered.

"Take your head out of the clouds and pin up another ad," her cousin said, pointing to a space on the advertising wall. While Priscilla kept their place in line, Kelsey did just that, then returned to the queue.

"What did Uncle Sander have to say about all this? I'm surprised he isn't out there helping you."

"Um, I haven't exactly told him that I've been on my own."

Priscilla stopped to give Kelsey a stern look. "Great. Now I have to tell Uncle Sander. He'll be upset if he learns that I knew and didn't say anything."

"No. Don't. Dad's busy with the search for the hidden family surprise." From when they were children, they had learned that Mark and Marlene had hidden a special treasure in Emerald Ridge before departing on their fateful trip to California.

Over the past twenty years, the Fortunes had looked everywhere for it on the family compound, but to no avail.

And they didn't even know *what* they were looking for. However, that August, during their yearly summer trip to Emerald Ridge from Dallas, her father, herself and her cousins vowed to stay there until they had found the surprise. She and her father had settled into the main house while her cousins had each moved into the guest cottages on the property that Mark and Marlene had built for each of their children. It was now November, and the family was still looking.

"Yeah. I'm not sure if my parents were just teasing about this long-lost family surprise, or if it's actually real. Before I moved out, I combed through my cottage but didn't find anything. It's been so long since my parents died, and I really hope this will be the year we find it. If we don't…" The sadness in her cousin's tone tugged at Kelsey's heart.

"I think it is." She tapped Priscilla's arm. "We'll find it. It's got to be *somewhere* on our property."

Priscilla released a long breath. "Between searching for the surprise and trying to figure out why Linc was killed, this has been one eventful summer." Linc Banning was the son of their childhood housekeeper who had been found shot to death in the Emerald Ridge River just before they came out to Emerald Ridge. That's when Priscilla revealed that she'd went out with Linc once, but he'd abruptly broke things off after that one date.

"Ugh. I don't have the bandwidth to talk about Linc Banning right now. I have such wonderful memories of Linc that I'm having a hard time processing the dark person he had become." Kelsey rubbed her temples. "I just hope they find who killed him."

Priscilla smiled. "Life has a funny way of working out sometimes. Jax is so wonderful that—"

"Yeah. Yeah. I'm going to cut you off before you start singing his praises." Kelsey chuckled. She had never been in love, but seeing Priscilla getting all gushy whenever she talked about her fiancé made her know she wanted to avoid it at all costs. Priscilla had fallen for Linc's stepbrother, Jax Wellington, the widowed father of a baby boy, Liam, and successful cattle rancher. "Let's circle back to my not having a foreman... If Dad hears that I fired Young, he might doubt my ability to run the ranch, and it's important to me to do this my way." When the other woman didn't look convinced, she pressed, "Give me until the end of the week and if I haven't hired anyone, I'll tell Dad myself."

"Alright. I can't resist those pleading green eyes. But make sure. Okay?"

"I will."

When they finished checking out, they stood off to the side of the register. The manager promised to have someone help her load her truck.

Priscilla's cell phone rang. "That's Jax. I'd better get going. I'm meeting him and Liam for lunch. But I'll ask him if he knows someone who can help you out."

"Thanks, I appreciate that." She sighed. Sometimes, she could be too hasty. But she would sleep good tonight. Kelsey battled insomnia whenever she was bothered about something, and she had been bothered about Young.

The cousins hugged and parted ways.

As Priscilla walked off, her phone pressed to her ear, Kelsey smiled. Her cousin was so happy. Kelsey felt a twinge of…what, exactly? *Loneliness*. She hadn't dated or had a serious relationship in a long time. But she was good with her decision. She had her business to focus on. So, she would redefine this feeling as restlessness and redirect her focus on… She looked around, her gaze falling to the stack of pumpkins outside the door. *Pumpkins*. She would bake a pumpkin pie.

Yes. That was a great way to fill her evening once she was done with her chores. Now she just had to find the perfect pumpkin. Small, dark, dense ones were the best for baking. She ran her hands along the hard fruit—or was it a vegetable? Spotting one under the pile, she moved the others out of the way to get to it.

Right as she picked it up in her hand, she heard loud wails from behind her. *Ear-piercing screams* were a more accurate description. Kelsey swung around so fast, her Stetson fell off her head, causing her long red curls to splay around her face. She was about to retrieve it off the ground, but was waylaid when she found herself locking eyes with the gorgeous man pushing the three babies in a wagon toward her.

For a second, she managed to tune out the screams to take in the man who, despite appearing to be overwhelmed, gave her a lopsided grin that said, *Help me.* She took a single step forward, her breath catching.

He was at least six foot three with skin the color of amber, a well-trimmed beard and black hair shaped into a sharp fade. Clearly he worked out because that T-shirt shaped his broad chest and abs in all the right places. As he drew close, her eyes dropped to his bare ring finger. Not that that meant anything. A lot of men didn't wear a wedding ring. She had no right checking out a man who was probably married, and who, based on his T-shirt, had his hands full with three babies.

Three *absolutely adorable* babies dressed in identical pumpkin suits, who were cute as could be despite their screams and the frowns of other shoppers giving him a wide berth.

Kelsey picked up her hat, dusted it off on her jeans and turned back to the pumpkins. She continued her search for another one fit for baking. Pies. She would focus on pies.

"C'mon guys," a low, deep voice a few feet behind her said. "Daddy is trying here. I just need five minutes to get some fruit and veggies, then we can go home. I promise." His words were soft and calm, but she could hear the slight frustration in his tone.

She snorted. Was he seriously trying to reason with

babies? The cries escalated. It was like they were riffing off each other. Poor guy didn't stand a chance. *Mind your business, Kelsey.* Grabbing another pumpkin, she moved toward the entrance to cash out. But his plea to his children stopped her.

"Help Daddy out, please."

Kelsey had never been able to resist a cry for help. Or children. She was a baby whisperer. In her family, her famed peekaboo was deemed magical. No baby could resist her charms, or so she had been told. She exhaled and looked upward. *Walk away. You don't have to do this.*

Oh, but of course, she did. Their cries were a siren.

Putting the produce back on the stand, she marched over to the melee and squatted beside the father. Her thighs bumped his, but she pretended not to notice the feel of those big, strong arms that moved to steady her, or those muscled thighs, and focused on the three little ones in front of her.

"Hello, there, little pumpkins," she sing-songed, touching each on their legs. Their father sat on the ground, the heat of his eyes on her, which she did her best to ignore right along with her suddenly frantic beating heart. She eyed the children's spiked lashes and the dried tears on their reddened cheeks, wishing she had more than two arms to bundle them all close to her.

Three little mouths hung open. Great. Now that she had their attention, it was time to seize the moment. She covered her eyes with her hands and then popped them open and squealed, "Peekaboo."

Hesitation.

She did it again. "Peekaboo!" Then a deep throated

chuckle from one and two tummies rumbled. Joy spread deep in her chest. How she loved hearing the sounds of children having fun. "Peeeekkkaboo!" she sing-songed.

This time there were three sets of giggles. As loud as they had been crying, they were now laughing. She cracked up and then faced their father. The look he gave her made her face heat.

"How did you do that?" he asked, amazed.

She shrugged to hide her reaction to his presence. He smelled of cedar and ocean and man. A combination that reminded her once more how long she had been alone. It had been six endless months since she'd been held by a man, and that brief encounter was best forgotten, tucked away into her never-shoulda-ever in this lifetime or the next. "I-I don't know. I just have a way with kids, I guess."

Grasping onto the stroller, she stood and dusted off her jeans. "Happy to have been of service. Have a great day!" She strutted off, pushing her hat deeper on her head. Then, spotting the helper by her flatbed, she gave a little wave.

"Wait!" She heard the distinct sound of wheels on the gravel, coming up alongside her.

"I'm sorry, but I can't let you leave like that. You were the heroine who stopped all the passersby cutting their eyes at me. I've got to repay you for your kindness," the man said, gracing her with a smile.

Oh, this one was quite the charmer. She had to remain immune even if her pulse wasn't beating like a rumba in her chest.

Gesturing to the associate to follow her, Kelsey said,

"You don't have to repay me." Then she saw one of her posted signs and tossed out, "Unless you happen to know some great ranch staff. I just bought a spread and I'm hiring but it's becoming a bit of a nightmare," she explained, not expecting that he would have a suggestion. They walked out to the parking lot, the helper lagging behind. "Which is why I am in desperate need of help."

"I don't know anyone, but I'm the owner of Porter Cuts in Dallas. Have you heard of it?" Of course she had.

"Who *hasn't*?" Kelsey stuck out her hand. "So, you must be..."

He grasped her hand, his touch warm and firm. Kelsey liked a man with a solid grip. "I'm Trevor Porter, and I'd be happy to give you tips on running a ranch and with staff management over dinner tonight, if you're available?"

"Uh, I'm Kelsey. Kelsey Fortune. I appreciate the offer but I've got a lot going on..."

"Fortune?" He raised a brow. "What a coincidence. My cousin's married to a Fortune."

"I would say it's a small world, but you can't sneeze without running into a Fortune here in Texas." She patted his arm. "Who is it?"

"Jonathan Porter, of the Porter Oil business. He's with Vivienne Fortune."

She whistled. "Yes, I heard about their wedding..."

"It's just dinner. We both have to eat, right? It's not a date."

The interest in his eyes and the energy between them contradicted his words.

She felt flustered, because she was so ready to say yes,

but then gave herself a much needed reality check. The man had *three* kids. Three. She opened the trunk and dug around in her bag for her purse and gave the associate a tip. She knew lifting those bags would be no easy feat.

"Hang on. Let me go help this dude while you think about it." He gave her a wink and jogged over to assist.

She played with the babies, stealing glances at Trevor's bulging muscles as he assisted with the load like they were a bag of feathers and not grain.

"So, what did you decide?" he asked once they were finished. "It's been the triplets, my dad and me since my wife's passing, but he's off on a cruise with his fiancé so it would be good to talk to someone who can respond with more than a babble."

"Happy to oblige… What made you move here?"

"I wanted to set up roots near family. I'm an only child and thought it would be nice to get to know my cousins, especially since I had the children. I would like them to have more family besides me and my pop."

She nodded. "I get it. I've got family all around me and we are ever growing. So, how will it work managing your company while you're here in Emerald Ridge? Do you plan to commute or will you get a new manager?" She felt her cheeks heat. "I'm sorry, my curiosity got away from me."

"No, don't apologize. Those are good questions. I have competent people working for me who oversee the day-to-day. But I weigh in on all the important decisions, conference in as needed and review meeting notes and updates, especially anything that involves the quality of our beef." He cleared his throat. "A lot of what I do now can be managed online, which leaves me time to spend with my family. The key was to recruit and train talented, loyal staff. Because of that, my company runs itself like a well-oiled machine."

She could use some pointers. "Well, I'm happy to learn from you later this evening. I live with my dad at the main house on the Fortune compound here in Emerald Ridge, though we both have our own wing. Have you heard of it?"

"Yes, I've heard of the estate, but I've never been."

She waved a hand. "Oh, it's hard to miss in this small town. I'll tell you all about its history when we meet. I'll cook us dinner." She rattled off her address and they exchanged numbers.

"I'm intrigued. I should have secured a sitter by this evening. See you about six tonight?"

"See you then."

Chapter Two

Trevor made his way down the winding driveway toward the Fortune compound, his eyes widening at the expanse of lush, green land before him. There were mini mansions along the estate, but the main house was straight ahead. From afar, it was a grand, imposing sight.

As he drew closer, his apprehension grew.

Maybe he should have canceled. Trevor peered at the three pairs of feet dangling from the car seats from his rearview mirror. They were each playing with their baby sheep, all toothy smiles. He wasn't sure how Kelsey would feel about him showing up with his children, but he wanted to see her again. For the first time in months, Trevor felt a spark of interest in another woman. A flame he had thought permanently doused after his wife's passing.

Neither had been ready for marriage but when Claudia discovered she was pregnant with the triplets, things shifted for the two of them, and they were willing to give their marriage another try for the children's sake.

But then, unexpectedly, Claudia was gone, and Trevor thought that was it for him as far as relationships. But now there was this buzz of excitement he'd felt when he'd met Kelsey earlier. He had to see if this was all a fluke or if this could be the start of a new chapter for him.

He glanced at the massive dwellings on either side of the path tucked away on the grounds. Each was beautifully landscaped with an air of understated elegance. If he recalled, his contractor had been an apprentice from the same company who designed these homes. His grip tightened on the steering wheel. After seeing the Fortune compound, Trevor couldn't wait to see the final results for his own home. So far, most of the updates had been via video call. He hadn't wanted to take the triplets with him around all the construction.

The main house lay ahead. His eyes drifted upward, taking it all in. The regal two-story sprawling structure boasted a sweeping roofline and massive columns. Kelsey texted she lived in the right wing, which had a separate entrance in the back, but since they were meeting for dinner, he should park by the front. With the baby bag on his shoulder, he removed the children from their car seats, gathered them in their wagon and hefted it up the three steps to the front door. Wiping his brow, Trevor paused to admire the wraparound porch, the large oak double doors and the wrought iron hinges before ringing the doorbell.

William started to fuss so Trevor bent over to rub his son's tummy until his boy gave him a toothy grin. After lunch and a nap, Trevor had changed the children into black pants and orange long-sleeved tees, while he had chosen a pair of black jeans and a long-sleeved tee for himself.

The creak of the door made him spin around.

Then he was looking into a pair of sparkling, green

eyes that made his breath catch. She had on a pair of jeans that showed off her curves and a billowy blouse.

"Hi..." She pointed to the children in the stroller and ran a hand through those silky strands. "Looks like you've got company."

"Yeah. The agency I use said the sitter took another job instead. I'm sorry. I was looking forward to meeting with you tonight and didn't want to cancel. But we can do this another time if bringing them was too much."

Moving past him, she squatted to greet his children. They immediately started wiggling and laughing.

There was a light breeze, and he enjoyed watching her vibrant red curls sway across her face. She was beautiful. And totally caught up in his children. What a way to man's heart. Er, if he were looking for a relationship.

Which of course he wasn't.

He had his hands full with his little bundles, and he couldn't expect another woman to willingly want that responsibility full-time.

After a few moments of playing with the children, she tilted her head to look at him, her smile genuine. "They are irresistible." He helped her to her feet and she murmured, "Come on, let's get inside."

Relaxing his shoulders, he grabbed the wagon's handle, willing himself to resist the sight of her perky butt in those jeans. "Lead the way."

They crossed the threshold into the foyer, and he peered up at the thirty-foot cathedral ceilings. The coos of his children created an echo, which only made them giggle and make louder sounds. He scanned the wide, airy flagstone entry that led into the living room, which featured a floor-to-ceiling fireplace on one side of the wall and plush, inviting couches. It was evident that the Fortunes didn't half step when it came to their abode. Huge bay windows gave a panoramic view of the property. He followed Kelsey, admiring the open floor plan, as they made their way into the kitchen, which extended into a sunken family area with a large television screen and bright-colored couches.

While they walked, Kelsey supplied a little back history. "This place once belonged to my Uncle Mark and his wife, Marlene. My dad's brother. They bought the place envisioning that it would be a summer estate for their family. Every time they had a child, they built them a home until it became what you see now."

"Oh, what a great idea," Trevor said, eyeing his own triplets. "I might steal that. I have more than enough space on my land to build three homes."

"Feel free to take pictures if you need inspiration," she offered.

"I might take you up on that." He winked. "I can just imagine the grand time your uncle and his wife had here. It seems as if they spared no expense."

They entered the kitchen. "Sadly, Mark and Melanie didn't live long enough to enjoy the fruits of their labor. They died in a plane crash," she said, her tone solemn.

"I'm sorry to hear that," Trevor said, resting his back against the quartz countertop. Sasha folded her legs to try to get out of the wagon and James had his arms outstretched.

"It's alright. It was a long time ago. Now it's just me and my dad here in the main house. We each have our own wing but we share the kitchen and living space." Eyeing the children, she waved a hand. "Give me a second. I'm pretty sure we have an oversize playpen somewhere that your children can roam about freely. There's too much trouble these little darlings can get into if we're not careful."

"Thanks, that would be wonderful. I didn't think to bring one, and I have three at home."

"It's all good," she said. "I'll be right back. Feel free to help yourself to whatever you like." She pointed to a large door. "We have everything you could want in the walk-in pantry."

He watched her retreat before taking in the kitchen. Wow. With the custom cabinetry, extra-large island and top-of-the-line appliances, it had everything a chef would dream of.

And then some.

Clearly, this was the heart of the home. He could tell that there had been a lot of love and laughter here because he felt the warmth in the atmosphere. A warmth that was reflected in Kelsey's green eyes…and made his insides get all twisted.

There were a couple Porter Cuts steaks defrosted on the countertop along with multicolored potatoes, onions, garlic and green peppers. The stove had a grill, but the day was nice enough to cook the food outside.

Trevor went to help himself to a bottle of water from the pantry. When he came back out and shut the door, the wagon was empty. His eyes went wide. He scurried around the room to see that William was crawling near the couch. James had opened a kitchen cabinet and

Sasha... Where was Sasha? He hadn't been gone but a second. How had those little rugrats gotten out so fast?

Picking up his sons, he asked, "Where's your sister?" Of course, they had no answer. James grabbed Trevor's hair, and William pulled on his dad's ears as they bounced in his arms.

Scurrying to find Sasha, Trevor peered into the dining room but there was no sign of her. His heart pounded in his chest. Not This house was huge and there were all kinds of places she could get into. Plus, there were stairs. *No! No! No!* Panicking, he bounded toward the foot of the staircase and peered up the winding stairs, his ears and eyes peeled. Then he scolded himself. Sasha wouldn't have gotten that far. Scuttling back, he retraced his steps, intending to go the direction that Kelsey had gone. That's when he heard a little laugh.

The ball in his stomach punctured from relief. "Sasha!" He moved toward the sound, calling out her name again.

Trevor stopped short. His baby girl was happily babbling in a man's arms, her hands on his cheeks. His protective instincts kicked in and he sped forward. "Hello, sorry about that. That's my daughter. She got away from me."

The older dude gave a laugh. "I see why. You've got your hands full. Literally. I'm Sander Fortune." Ah. The owner. Kelsey's dad. She must have gotten her height, red hair and green eyes from her mother because Sander looked like he was over six feet and he had blond hair and blue eyes. Sander cocked his head. "And you are?" The gentleman's tone was mildly curious, and he didn't look alarmed, as if he bumped into a stranger in his house all the time. Wait, did he?

"I'm Trevor. Kelsey's...uh, friend." He rushed to explain. "She went to search for a playpen."

"Oh, yes. She told me you would be here. She's probably in the attic getting it." Sander rubbed Sasha's tummy, and then they made their way back to the kitchen. "I found this cutie heading for the bathroom."

"Thank you. It's great meeting you."

"Welcome. We're pretty laid-back here. So make yourself at home. Did my daughter give you a tour yet?"

"No, not yet. I only arrived a few minutes ago."

Sasha held out her arms for Trevor to take her, but of course, he had his hands full. She started to fuss. "Give me a second, sweetheart." He placed William and James in the wagon and picked up the baby bag to give them their pacifiers and a stuffed toy. That should keep them satisfied for a few moments. Where on earth was Kelsey?

As if he had voiced the question aloud, she returned with a huge box in hand. "I'm back. I had to trudge up to the attic for the playpen. Did you get my text?" She looked over at her father, who still held Sasha in his arms. "Oh, hey, Dad. I'm guessing you two have already introduced yourselves."

"Yes," Sander said, handing over Sasha to Trevor before giving his daughter a peck on her cheek. "I was just about to head over to Roth's when I saw this adorable baby doll coming my way."

"She might have been following you, Kelsey," Trevor told her as he rubbed Sasha's back. The baby rested her face against his chest. All the frazzled emotions melted away at her sweet little face.

"We're about to cook dinner. Did you want me to save you something?" Kelsey asked her dad.

"No thanks," Sander said. "I'm having a bite with Roth."

Nodding, she went three steps down into the sunken family room and began to unpack the box in a corner of the room. She looked relaxed, the exact opposite of how he felt.

"Let me help you with that," Sander offered. The two made quick work of assembling the playpen, so with Kelsey's permission, Trevor busied himself by taking the steaks out of their wrapping and prepping them for seasoning. He also washed the vegetables and potatoes.

The children could eat mashed potatoes, and he'd ask Kelsey if they could boil some carrots to go with it. The triplets each had six teeth—three on top, and three on bottom—in the same places. The wonder of triplets.

Kelsey and her dad kept up a steady stream of low conversation, centered around figuring out how to get things set up. Trevor was moved by Sander's graciousness. He could see where Kelsey inherited her warmth. He thought of his own father and sent Orson a text to check on him. Sander left the room, briefly returning with a basket of toys. Of course, that led to three excited shrieks. Trevor grinned, wiped his hands on the kitchen towel and walked around the island to peek at them as they bounced around excitedly in the playpen.

He snapped a pic. They looked so cute he couldn't resist.

"There. That should occupy them while you two talk

business." Sander brushed his hands on his legs. "Kelsey tells me that you're here to give her some tips with the ranch. That's nice of you. She's determined to do it without me, so I'm glad to see she's accepting advice from someone."

"I'm glad to help."

"Daddy, don't you have somewhere to be?" Kelsey said, her tone pointed, communicating that her father had outstayed his welcome. Communicating that perhaps this was *more* than a business meeting? Trevor straightened. Hmm. *Invigorated* was the word that best described the feeling now coursing through his veins.

"Right. Yes." Sander observed them for a beat, then tipped his hat and went to say goodbye to the children before addressing him with an, "I'll see you around." It wasn't cold, but it wasn't warm either. It was more like… guarded. The kind of tone from a dad who knows when his daughter is into someone.

Trevor and Kelsey stood facing each other, as the click of Sander's boots echoed throughout, the sound of the door closing filling the quiet.

Kelsey broke eye contact, moved away from Trevor and turned on the television in the kitchen. She surfed through the channels before putting on *Bluey*.

The three babies clapped their hands. "Are they hungry?" she asked, changing topics.

"They are okay for now. I fed them a snack before we came over. In about an hour or so, they will be ready to eat though."

She began working on the steaks. "So, how long have you been raising your children on your own?"

"Claudia—their mother—passed not too long after they were born, so it's pretty much been me and them ever since. I took a year off from work to care for them. My father helps but is away on a cruise, and so I've been looking for a temporary stand-in but I haven't found anyone suitable." He jutted his chin in the direction of where they sat watching television. "Someone with not just the skill but also the patience." He shrugged. "I'll know when I meet them."

She glanced over at the children whose eyes were glued to the screen. Gosh, they were so darned cute. If only she could volunteer her services, but she had a lot going on at the ranch already.

Perhaps if she had a foreman, she could juggle her schedule and help pitch in. Speaking of which...she *really* needed to get someone hired. Hopefully, one of her interviewees tomorrow would be the person.

Kelsey fired up the indoor grill and turned on the fan above the stove. Then she reached for her cast-iron skillet to sear the meat and turned on the burner. Normally, she would use the outdoor grill, but she didn't want to be going back and forth, leaving Trevor with the children inside, and the temperatures were going to dip about ten degrees. She couldn't chance any of the triplets getting sick.

He pointed at the potatoes and green peppers. "Do you want me to chop those for you? I make a great sous chef." With a nod, she retrieved a knife and a chopping board. "That would be great...thanks."

"I'm on it. Also, if you have three carrots, I can prepare that for the children."

"Sure." She grabbed some out of the refrigerator and handed them to him.

Trevor saluted and got to work.

While the skillet heated, Kelsey dropped some butter inside, then diced the onion and garlic before adding some to the butter. She placed the meat inside the skillet, having already seasoned it with salt and pepper.

"That smells good," Trevor said, sniffing the air.

"Thanks. It's quality meat." She winked at him before shuffling off to get the potatoes. She liked how things were so easy, so familiar, between the two of them. It was like she had known him for years instead of hours. Heart skittering, she handed him the fork. "Let's have it sear on both sides while I'll put these potatoes on to boil."

"At your service, ma'am." Their fingers grazed when he took the utensil out of her hand, and she swore she had more steam inside her than the meat on the stove. The energy between them was surprising.

And *tantalizing*.

Sucking in a breath, Kelsey asked, "How do you like your steak?"

"Medium well."

"Me too."

"You mentioned it was just you and your dad here. May I ask where your mother is?" Trevor asked, flipping the meat.

"My mom died in a car accident when I was a month old."

The fork fell out of Trevor's hand with a clink. "Wow. I'm sorry. I had no idea."

"It's okay. You didn't know. But when you told me that your wife had passed, I felt an instant kinship with your kids because I too grew up without a mom." She released a quavering breath. "It wasn't easy and I think of her often, wondering what she would say, what she would think of me now. Stuff like that. But my father has been great, which helped." She pointed his way. "Like you seem to be with your children."

"I try. But I have a lot to learn. Being a father is the most scary but wonderful thing in the world."

Kelsey smiled. "I can imagine. I don't know what I would do without my dad. He's my biggest supporter, and we have a great relationship."

"I hope to have the same with my children." Their eyes met for a beat before Trevor cleared his throat. He took out the steak and rested it in the baking tin, then placed the other to brown. "I do wonder how I'll handle the void of the mother being in their life."

She lifted her chin and met his gaze. "Just love them. You'll make mistakes. My dad isn't perfect, but his love for me is and it's all I ever needed." She gave a little laugh. "Along with some good aunts and uncles and cousins. Family is important."

"I agree. That's why I sought out my father once I learned that I was having triplets. My mother didn't tell me about Pop until she was on her deathbed."

"Whoa. Maybe she had her reasons?"

"Maybe. But I was too focused on her deteriorating

health to ask too many questions. I mainly let her talk while I listened."

"Do you have more family besides your dad and cousin?"

"Yes, but none that I care to know." The edge in his tone told Kelsey not to push or ask questions. She would learn more in time.

They continued to work side by side in companionable silence, the aroma of the food cooking making her mouth water. Once everything was prepared, they tag-teamed it and fed the children the mashed potatoes and carrots. Then he dug in their baby bag for their sippy cups, which they filled with formula. She shifted the conversation by asking Trevor to give her some tips on securing a foreman and ranch hands who would take her seriously.

Trevor told her that it was all about passion and being confident in her abilities. Instead of asking them if they could do things, she needed to assert her authority from the very beginning and be firm instead of tentative. Kelsey accepted his advice and vowed to do it the next day with her interviewees. She wished she could offer him advice on actually finding a babysitter, but she didn't have any children of her own. A few hours with her baby cousins did not an expert make.

By then the children had conked out, so they ate in the dining room. They enjoyed their food under candlelight, and then together they washed the pots and stacked the dishwasher. They kept bumping hips, here and there, which kept her body in overdrive. It was close to 9:00 p.m. when they huddled on the couch, with the only sound besides their chatter being the hum of the dishwasher.

All in all, this made for a very nice evening, and she told him so.

He moved closer to run his fingers through her hair. "Kelsey, I'd like to kiss you, if that's okay."

She scooted close to him. "If that's okay? I thought you'd *never* ask." Then she cupped his face with her hands and planted her lips onto his.

He took charge of the kiss and whispered in her ear, "I've been dying to do that all evening." That low rumble in her ear was her undoing. She rocked her hips, and he deepened the kiss.

When he tore his lips away, she exhaled. "That was some first kiss." His mouth was lipstick stained from their kisses.

He wiped the perspiration off his brow and locked eyes with her. "When I started my day this morning, this wasn't how I imagined it ending."

She smiled. "I didn't either."

He looked at his watch. "It's pretty late. I'd better get going…" They shared another brief kiss.

This time she broke free and stood to put distance between them. "I'll help you get the children out to your truck," she whispered. "Hopefully, we won't wake them." She was almost tempted to tell Trevor to leave them until the morning, but then reality kicked in. There was no way she was ready to tackle three babies at night.

Trevor went outside to start up the truck and stow the wagon and baby bag. Meanwhile, she gathered Sasha into her arms, inhaling the little girl's scent. Knowing that this precious child would never know what it felt like to have a mother's arm wrapped about her broke Kelsey's heart. She knew what it was like to experience puberty, to have all those questions, without a mother's touch. Or guidance. She also knew what it was to never experience love from one of the people that mattered most. The thought of Sasha, William and James experiencing the same pain she had was just too much. Kelsey squeezed her eyes shut to keep the tears at bay. She felt ridiculous getting emotional when just yesterday she hadn't even known of their existence.

But all it took was one day and she was already attached. Smitten. She didn't want to see these babies leave. Even now, as Trevor came back inside and lifted William out of the playpen, she dreaded their departure. But he would probably snatch them and run for the hills if she told him how deeply connected she felt to his children.

"Kelsey?" she heard from behind her. "You okay?" She turned around to face Trevor, who had his arms open.

Instinctively, she drew Sasha closer. He arched a brow. "I can walk her out then wait with the children while you come back for James." She could feel his eyes on her as she headed toward the car. He must be wondering about her sudden mood shift, but if she divulged what she was thinking, there was no doubt he would question her sanity.

Chapter Three

He had no business kissing Kelsey last night. She was only twenty-five. Yes, that was a mere six years younger than his own age, but it was a lifetime of difference when it came to experience. He had already been married, was now a widower, and now he was juggling fatherhood. She was just starting out.

That's why at daybreak, while preparing oatmeal for the kids, Trevor had convinced himself that the best thing he could do for Kelsey Fortune was stay away from her. He had too much baggage.

She was beautiful. Inside and out. And could have her pick in men. Why would she be interested in him and his ready-made family? Yes, last night was amazing and the most fun he'd had with a woman in well over a year, but he had to be real with himself before he got in over his head with Kelsey. Because he could.

Quite easily.

If he allowed it. So, the answer was simple. Stay away from her. Turning off the burner, Trevor put the oatmeal to cool. Then he got to washing and cutting apples before pureeing them in his baby food blender.

At precisely six-thirty, his doorbell rang.

That would be his potential new nanny. She had answered his ad through email when he got home last night, and they had agreed for her to arrive before the triplets awakened. That way they could have an actual conversation without the usual chaos. He smiled and padded to the front door.

"Hello," she smiled, her chin high. "I'm Cindy."

Trevor liked that, though it was early in the morning, the woman looked refreshed and upbeat, and she radiated confidence. That was a good sign. According to her résumé, she had experience working with multiples and she had even been in charge of a day care center, which made him hopeful that he had found the one.

"Hello, Cindy," he greeted, stepping aside. "Come on in."

They headed to the kitchen, and she slipped onto the bar stool behind the counter, folding her hands in front of her. Now that he had a good look at her, she looked young, but he didn't want to ask her age. She was dressed in jeans and a sweater and had her dark brown hair swept up in a ponytail. But her oversize trendy glasses took up most of her face.

"So, I checked your references and they gave you such glowing reviews, which put my mind at ease. But can you tell me why you're seeking this position? From your résumé, I'm surprised you're even available." Grabbing three bowls, he ladled the oatmeal inside and then reached for the applesauce, placing generous amounts inside.

"I'm in between jobs at the moment so I've started doing temporary nannying. I have gotten to travel throughout Europe as an extra hand for parents who want to get away but don't want to leave their babies. Although I like the experience, I am on the hunt for something more permanent. Something stable so I can attend night classes." She pushed her glasses up on her face.

"That sounds like a great plan."

Her chest puffed. "My goal is to graduate from college debt-free." Trevor loved that she had a plan for her future. His optimism rose.

"Awesome. Well, I'm not sure if the agency informed you, but you would begin on a trial basis. My triplets are at the age where they are active and into everything, so I want to see how you do. I have some work to take care of in my office, but I'll be here if you need me." Plus he had already turned on the nanny cam so he would be able to keep an eye on things from his office.

"Yes, the agency informed me that the trial would be part of the interview process. I get that as you want to make sure we're a good fit. I'm sure I'll be fine."

Just then, a soft cry came through the baby monitor on the counter along with some rustling. Then another cry. And another. "And they're up."

She shot to her feet. "And so am I." Holding up a hand, Cindy assured him. "I've got this."

"Alright." Baby monitor in hand, Trevor showed her where everything was inside the pantry and then took her into their bedroom, which was an oversize master that he had converted into a nursery for three. He had converted another room into their official playroom, but more times than not, he found himself setting them in the living room. The kitchen was already filled with their paraphernalia. Basically, every room besides his office and his bedroom had become their domain.

He had chosen a Noah's ark theme for the nursery, and the walls were painted a light gray with white trimmings. The three cribs took up a good portion of the room, but he had two rocking chairs and a large center rug. There were three changing stations, and three gigantic teddy bears in the corners that Claudia had insisted on buying. He chuckled now thinking of that before his smile dimmed.

"Wow. This place is great," Cindy said, going over to where William stood, shaking the crib bars. Sasha had a leg propped over hers, and James sat eating his bed sheet.

"Thank you. My late wife and I put a lot of thought into it." They each took a child and began changing diapers. "I like to have breakfast ready for when they get up, and then in a couple hours, I give them a morning snack. I have typed out a schedule for you to follow. It's on the refrigerator."

"Okay, thanks."

Finishing up with Sasha, he scooped up James next. Trevor frowned. James's cheeks appeared to be a little red, but it could be because he had been crying. He was about to check if the little guy had a temperature when his cell phone buzzed.

It was a text from Hammond. What on earth did his grandfather want now? He looked down at the message. *I have a good sitter if you need one while your father is away.*

With a grunt, he deleted the text and shoved his phone in his pocket. His cousin must have told Hammond about his father's trip and Trevor's need for a babysitter. Jonathan had been encouraging him to give his grandfather another chance, saying life was too short. But all Trevor could think about was how Hammond had snubbed his mother. Trevor had watched his mother suffer alone on her deathbed when she could have had family by her side, and it was all Hammond Porter's doing. There was no forgetting that for him. Ever.

His cell rang. This time it was Kelsey. Despite his earlier vow to keep his distance from her, he couldn't hold back a smile.

"You could go ahead and get going if you need to, Mr. Porter. I've got this." Cindy bounced James in her arms.

"Are you sure?" he asked, looking at his phone. He wanted to answer before it went to voicemail.

"Yes."

"Okay, call if you need." He put the phone to his ear. "Hey, Kelsey, what's going on?" She was frantic, shouting something about losing sheep and she didn't know who else to call. Trevor didn't understand what she was saying, but he knew he had to get to her. He rushed to grab his jacket and checked to make sure the video feed on his app was working. "I'll be right over."

How did they get out?

She had asked herself that question numerous times since coming out early that morning to feed the sheep. There were only three of them in the field and her two sheep dogs were missing and the door to the barn was unlocked. What she wasn't sure of was whether one of the men she had fired had done this or if she had been so busy rehashing her hot kissing session with Trevor that she had forgotten to close the barn door before.

Heaving a long sigh, Kelsey had called Jax, but he didn't pick up. He was probably out in the field tending to his own cattle. She'd left him a message and then jumped into her truck and drove the perimeter of her ranch but didn't see them. Shielding her eyes against the rising sun, there'd been nothing but road and land in sight. Where on earth had they gotten off to? She tried reaching Priscilla next, but her cousin didn't respond either.

So, out of options, she'd decided to call Trevor as a last resort.

Lord, she could *just imagine* if Young were still here, he would have blasted this all over social media. She would be a laughingstock once again. Truth was, she was horrified at her mistake.

But Trevor hadn't laughed at her predicament. In fact, when she'd sent him an SOS, he'd simply said, "I'll be right over," and her knees had literally weakened with relief.

After texting him the address for the ranch, she rushed into the main building and into the restroom to wash her face and hands. Next she dragged a brush through her tresses. A thought occurred and her eyes went wide. *The triplets!* If Trevor showed up with them, how would that work?

The main building had a small, stark reception area, her office, the bathroom and another office that doubled for storage. She didn't have any space for the children to move about. This wasn't a safe space for them, and even if Trevor had his wagon, Kelsey didn't see them staying confined.

However, she needn't have worried. Trevor came alone. When she opened the door and saw him in his red flannel shirt, blue jeans, boots and cowboy hat, her breath caught. This man was fine as all get-out. She avoided looking him in the eyes or he might see the want in hers. "Where's the children?" she croaked out, her hand circling her neck. Gosh, she needed a drink of water.

He leaned against the doorjamb. "They're at home. I have a new nanny I am trying out." He held up his cell phone. "I have a security system and I can view them on my phone." He crooked his head at the truck. "How about we go find some sheep?"

"Yes, I'd like that." Trevor opened the passenger door to his truck.

"I've already circled the property, but I didn't see or hear them anywhere."

Starting up the truck and backing out one of the two spots in front of the main building, he asked, "Do you have water nearby?"

"A small creek, but it's near the edge of my ranch. To be precise, it's on the bordering property. There's a shortcut." She pointed to the patch of flattened earth, and Trevor turned in that direction.

"We'll head there."

"Okay, but I doubt we'll find them there. It's all fenced in."

He shot her a quick glance. "Any chance that someone tampered with it?"

"No, I checked. Everything appears to be in order. I didn't notice they were gone right away because I started my day in the other two barns."

She tensed, waiting for him to make some disparaging remark, but Trevor merely nodded.

"Hang on. Slow down for a minute. If you go too fast, we'll miss the shortcut." Squinting, she leaned forward. "There it is. Make a sharp turn there."

The minute he cleared the brushes, she saw them. The dogs. *And* the sheep. Calmly lapping by the waters. Her cheeks warmed as relief flooded her body. "I didn't think to check down here."

"Always start with water."

Between the two of them, they led the dogs and sheep back to her property. She checked the pregnant ewes, relieved to see that they were unharmed from their adventure. This time Kelsey made sure to secure the fence. Then Trevor helped her with the other chores. He was such a thoughtful man. And hardworking. He tossed the hay and feed like it was a bag of packing peanuts. Once the chores were done, they walked back to the main building. Kelsey found she wasn't ready to part ways. Since the children were with a sitter, she could use this opportunity to get to know Trevor better. "Whew. Thank you so much for coming over. How about I make you breakfast as a thank you."

"You don't have to…"

"I have to eat anyway," she insisted.

"Sure. If it isn't too much trouble." He patted his midriff. "My stomach is already thanking you in advance. I left without eating breakfast." They caravanned the five miles back to the Emerald Ridge Fortune estates and pulled up to the main house. Her father's usual parking spot was empty. Good. If he were there, he might suspect she was interested in Trevor and put the man through an inquisition. Trevor came around to open her door and helped her out of the truck. She appreciated the gentlemanly gesture. Of course, then her foot twisted slightly, and she ended up falling into his arms, her hand clutching his shirt against that strong, firm chest.

"Easy now," he rumbled, his voice in her ear.

Tilting her head, she looked into those sultry brown eyes. Desire flowed in their depths, echoing the attraction swirling in her lower regions. She swallowed. Being close to this man was intoxicating.

Flustered, she righted herself. "I'm sorry about that. I'm not usually such a klutz."

"No problem. I can scratch having a fine woman like yourself fall into my arms off my bucket list."

She gave him the side-eye but couldn't stop the smile tugging at her lips as she opened the door. While Trevor popped into the restroom, Kelsey grabbed six eggs—fresh from her farm—and a package of turkey bacon. She eyed the slices of sharp cheddar cheese before taking it out along with a tomato and some spinach. She would make omelets instead. There were still some of the breakfast potatoes that would be a nice accompaniment to her meal.

After washing her hands, she placed the bacon in the air fryer and began whisking the eggs. Trevor came into the kitchen.

"What can I do?"

"How about you dice the tomato for me?" She told him where to find the chopping board and the knife.

She loved how at ease he was with her in her home. The handful of men she had dated before had been intimidated by her father's wealth and her luxurious surroundings. She scoffed. Or maybe it was Sander's questions about their lifelong plans that had scared them off. She reached for her cast-iron pan and turned the burner on low.

Just then, Trevor's cell phone went off. He did a quick check, tightened his lips and then shoved his phone in his pocket. "Everything alright?" she asked.

"Yeah. Yeah." Yet his body appeared rigid, and his brows had furrowed. The poor tomato—he was chopping away at it like it had done him something wrong. Apparently the man had some aggression to work out.

Was that another woman texting? If that were the case, well, that was *none* of her business. They weren't dating, she reminded herself. In fact, they hadn't even passed the twenty-four-hour mark yet since they'd met. She gave the eggs another firm whisk until they fluffed.

Still, inexplicable jealousy furled in her gut. *Quit it.* She poured half of her egg mix into her pan and added salt and pepper, before adding the cheese and spinach.

"The tomato is ready."

"Thanks." She added it to the omelets. "Breakfast will be ready in a jiffy."

"Cool." His phone rang again. This time he answered, putting the phone on speaker. "Hey, Cindy, is everything alright over there?"

"No, these babies are way too much for me! One of the

boys grabbed my hair and Sasha bopped me on the nose. I have a serious nosebleed. I'm sorry, I can't do this."

"Can you give me about a half hour?"

"Is that the soonest you can get here?"

Oh, Lord. The sitter sounded frazzled. Kelsey tapped Trevor's shoulder. "Go get them. Bring them here."

"You sure?"

"Yes. Positive."

Trevor gave Kelsey a thumbs-up and mouthed a thank-you, before telling Cindy, "I'm on my way."

Chapter Four

His kitchen could be declared a hazard zone. He was going to have to pay his housekeeper double her usual fee to get the place back in order, and it would be worth every dollar.

Food was scattered everywhere, and somehow oatmeal and apples had ended up on the walls. There was also a faint burnt smell in the air. Perhaps Cindy had tried to cook something? The blackened pan left no clue as to what it was.

Cindy had been waiting at the door and all but shoved William into his arms before departing to get her nose looked at. Her clothes and hair were covered in food. And her glasses had been cracked and were now in her pocket. Not even his offer to pay the woman for the day and for her medical expenses had mollified her. He was pretty sure it wasn't broken though, but it was bleeding. Despite the mess, his children only needed minor cleaning with a baby wipe.

If it weren't for the fact that Kelsey had made breakfast, Trevor would have stayed put, but she was expecting his return. So he left a note of apology for his housekeeper, along with a generous payment, packed up the car with a few toys and the baby bag then headed back to Kelsey's.

When he pulled up, he found her waiting, which was a great relief. The playpen was still up, they put the children inside. As soon as he stepped inside and smelled all that good food, his tummy growled. Kelsey chuckled.

"You heard that?" he asked.

"Yeah. Go on and help yourself. I'll get the children settled."

"What about you?"

"I nibbled on some bacon, so I'll hold for a few."

"Okay, thanks." Trevor placed an omelet, some of the potatoes from the night before and a couple pieces of bacon on his plate and popped it in the microwave. If the food tasted as good as it smelled, his mouth was going to be very happy.

Meanwhile, she went outside, returning with the toys and the baby bag. Trevor took that moment to thank her for cooking and also for opening her home to him and his triplets once again.

"It's not a problem at all," she said, her cheeks rosy. The microwave beeped, and he retrieved his steaming plate before placing hers inside. She came over to where he stood, and he inhaled the faint smell of apples. Her dampened hair indicated that she had taken a shower while he was gone. She had changed into a pair of sweats with a matching pullover hoodie.

"Do you want coffee or OJ?" she asked, her pert nose tilted in the air.

"OJ is fine, thanks," he said, dragging his eyes from those cute polished toes peering out from under her pants. He sat at the island, facing the children, and dug into his meal. He heard the beep of the microwave and then the next thing he knew, her warm body was next to his.

When they both had finished their plates clean, she dragged her chair close to him and whispered, "How was everything back at your house?" That's when he saw that James was lying down in the playpen. Poor guy must have fallen asleep.

"It was a disaster. The kitchen looked like it had been hit by a tornado, and Cindy flew through the door with her bloody nose. I'm not sure how or why, but she looked a hot mess while the children pretty much were intact."

Sasha and William were busy playing with their teddy bears, but they would probably be ready for some downtime as well. The triplets usually took two naps daily. A short one before lunch and a longer one before dinner. He couldn't let them sleep too long though or getting them to bed would be a nightmare.

Kelsey chuckled. "That is hilarious." She took a sip of orange juice.

"Her bloody nose?"

"No, the part where you said she looked worse than the children."

"I wish I had taken a picture." He laughed, but his humor instantly faded when he heard James moaning. Dropping his fork, Trevor went to check on his son. He reached over and touched James's forehead. It felt a little warm. Turning the baby over, Trevor could see his face was now flushed. Oh no. James was probably sick—or maybe breaking in a new tooth. He prayed it was the latter.

"Do you have a thermometer in the baby bag?" Kelsey asked, placing a hand on his back. Her voice held concern that sounded...*motherly*. He tensed for a moment. His children would never have that.

Trevor nodded. "Yes, it's in the front pocket in the first aid kit. I never leave home without it. Because you just never know."

With a soft smile, Kelsey went to get the thermometer.

He picked up James in his arms and went to sit on the couch. Of course, William and Sasha wanted to be held too. But he put the television on to distract them. While he took James's temperature, Kelsey played with William and Sasha. Grief that Claudia wasn't here for them hurt his heart. Things between them might have been shaky but he had truly loved her and knew she would have made a good mother. That just made him appreciate Kelsey's kindness even more.

Yet worry swarmed. He didn't know how he was going to juggle caring for a sick child while giving the other two the attention they deserved. But he didn't want to take advantage of Kelsey, who had her hands full running the ranch, so he had better get going.

The thermometer beeped. His shoulders slumped. No fever. What a relief. Trevor opened James's mouth, grinning as his little head lolled. Sure enough, his lower right gums were reddened. Cradling James against him, Trevor gave him some pain reliever and kissed James's forehead. "You'll feel better in no time, buddy." He turned to Kelsey. "I'm going to get out of your hair. James might be a little cranky and I don't want to impose on you any longer."

"Nonsense." She came over and placed her hands on

her hip. "You're not going anywhere." His head snapped up at her bossy tone. "I have a proposition for you. What if we help each other out?"

He placed James next to him. "What are you suggesting?"

"You can help me get the ranch going and I can help care for the triplets?"

"Come again?"

"I didn't stutter."

He folded his arms, holding back a smile at her spunky response. "Can you elaborate?"

She drew in a breath. "I have a few guest rooms on my side of the house. You and the triplets can stay here until you've secured a sitter."

It took a moment for her words to register. But once they did, Trevor jumped to his feet and placed his hands on each of her arms. "Are you *sure* about that?"

"Yeah…"

"How would it work since you have your ranch and I have my company?"

"We'll figure it out."

"Okay… What would your father say?"

"My dad loves children. He'll be more than fine. Trust me." She grinned. "In fact, he'll thank you for stepping up to help me with the ranch. He's barely here anyway. He's a ranch architect and sometimes he's on the road looking at undeveloped land or redesigning ranches. And if he isn't working, he's doing classes or events. Like right now, I got him into pickleball."

The idea took root in his mind. It was a great plan. And they both would benefit. "I love it. Would you be okay with us staying until the end of the month? I'd give up the rental since the lease is ending anyway, and then I'd just move from here into my house."

"That makes sense. Yes, that would be fine."

"Okay, thank you so much for opening your home to us." He hesitated. "But I have one condition."

She arched a brow. "Which is…?"

"That you explain to your father that this is temporary. I don't want him to think I'm taking advantage."

"Fine, but I assure you, Dad won't think that way. Besides, you're the owner of Porter Cuts and I'm pretty sure he knows you can afford to live where you want."

"Alright. If you're sure."

"I am. I also have my own entrance in the back so you can come and go as you please. But you're more than welcome to use the front door." She was all smiles.

"I do have one more question." He cleared his throat. "Since we'll be…uh…living under the same roof, how do you see things playing out between us? After that kiss we shared, I'm sure it's no secret that I'm attracted to you."

She twirled a lock of hair around her finger. "The feeling is mutual, but I see what you're getting at…" She mulled it over for several moments. "Maybe it would be best if we slow things down and let this thing between us…*whatever* it is…fold out naturally?"

"I don't want to halt things entirely, but I do agree that we can just see how it goes. Maybe not feel pressured to put a definition on what we have? I *could* use a friend. We could build on that." That was a very adult approach.

Even as he said that, Trevor wasn't completely convinced he could be so laid-back, so fluid about such an intense connection, but the fact that he had three children was something that had to be considered deeply. On both their parts.

She stuck out a hand. "Friends it is."

"Let's shake on it." He held out his hand. "I'll call the movers and a professional cleaning service." Their hands joined before he drew her in for a hug. "Thank you, Kelsey. You won't regret this."

"Of course I won't," she said, peering up at him. "We have the most perfect arrangement. What could go wrong?"

Straddled astride Kahlua, one of her brown mares, Kelsey galloped to the edge of her property by the maple trees where her sheep grazed and pulled on the reins. The mare came to a smooth stop.

She snatched off her Stetson and shook her hair as it settled on her shoulders. Placing her hat on her thigh, Kelsey drew in a deep breath and tilted her face to the wide-open sky to soak in the evening sun. This was her favorite time of day. Right as the sun was disappearing below the horizon.

A light breeze tickled her face, and she closed her eyes for a few seconds, welcoming the peace.

Adjusting her horse, Kelsey turned around to scan the lush green pastures, her heart filled with pride. Thanks to input from her cousin Jax Wellington, who was operating his own spread, Liam's Lone Star Ranch, on the other side of Emerald Ridge, she had begun to practice rotational grazing to promote healthy grass. So now, pride filled her chest as her sheep ate contentedly while they awaited the arrival of their lambs.

She wiped at the small bead of sweat lining her forehead and massaged her shoulders. She had just finished cleaning out the barn where she housed the sheep. Her arms were sore from lifting and hoisting the hay bedding and she had been relieved that she hadn't encountered any rodents during her chore.

Running a ranch was hard, taxing, but the rewards were worth it. There was the sound of a truck approaching on the gravel path beyond the fence. Recognizing the driver, she gave a little wave and dismounted, securing her mare against a tree.

"Hey, Jax. I didn't know you were coming by today," she called out once he was within hearing distance.

He got out of the vehicle and walked over to where she stood. "I got your message about your sheep getting out yesterday morning. When I didn't hear from you, I figured you found other assistance. But I came by to see if you needed a hand. Priscilla filled me in on your staffing situation."

"Yeah. Yesterday was an ordeal. But as you can see, all is well. Luckily, I had a friend available to help me out." Trevor had called in a few of his workers and his cousin Jonathan to help out on her ranch while they searched for permanent workers. Kelsey was grateful for that because then she and Trevor had been able to devote their energy to minding the triplets before she left for the ranch. "I'm sorry I didn't think to text you and update you."

"That's alright." He jutted his chin toward the grass.

"Is it time to move the sheep?" he asked. Jax was the one who had helped Kelsey set up the land for grazing. They moved the sheep to another section of land every twenty-one days.

"I'll give it another few days then I'll move them."

"Alright. I'll be by if you need."

"Thanks. But hopefully, I won't." She settled her hat on her head and tucked her hair in a bun. "I'm conducting interviews later today so if all goes well, I should have a new foreman this evening."

"That sounds wonderful. Just let me know if you need more ranch hands, and I'll send you help."

"I will." With a wave, he was gone. She glanced at her watch and her eyes went wide. Where had the time gone? She scurried back to her horse. She had to get back to the main house. Kelsey could not be late for this interview.

"Nancy Sherwood has excellent references and she's been in the business for close to fifteen years," Kelsey said, looking over the details of their last applicant scheduled for the end of the day. If this interview ended the way she hoped, she would finally be able to get some sleep.

She and Trevor sat around the kitchen table while the triplets played as they conducted interviews using video conferencing. Though she could have handled the interviews without Trevor, Kelsey was glad Trevor was there to give input on the hire.

And so far, Trevor had been a great interview partner. He took copious notes on all the interviewees, and Kelsey appreciated how serious he was about finding her foreman. Once she had the foreman, then that person would be responsible for staffing the ranch, though Kelsey would have final hiring approval.

"I agree. Nancy has a great track record. I would hire her myself if I needed a foreman." Trevor placed a hand on her leg. A move that distracted her.

"I've got to add that I love that she's a woman." Kelsey shifted her leg, and he moved his hand. She felt the loss but now she could concentrate on the task at hand. Because that hand had been like fire on her leg, its heat spreading to her lower regions.

Trevor nodded. "A *competent* woman." A statement proven true once they had interviewed the forty-year-old brunette. She had a soft voice and firm demeanor that commanded respect.

Kelsey was so impressed, she only had one question. "When can you start?" Then she disclosed what was a competitive annual salary and outlined the benefits, which included healthcare, dental and vision plans. Kelsey had done her research and knew what she offered was more than ample. "There's also an end-of-year bonus if we meet our annual targets."

"Wow, that figure is more than generous. I'm pleased to accept the position. Six weeks would be ideal so I can give proper notice and find lodging for me and my son. We don't have a lot of possessions, but finding an affordable place is usually my biggest challenge," Nancy said, running a hand through her tresses. "Nathan's almost twenty and makes for a good ranch hand. He graduated high school early and has a finance degree but prefers working with his hands."

"Your young man sounds impressive. I'll prepare a compensation package for him as well if he's interested. No need to go house hunting. This job comes with accommodations—the main house on the Fortune 8 ranch. It has two master suites, so there's more than enough room for you and your son. If you don't mind living in one of the cabins for now. I'll work on getting the main house renovated to your style. But I'll send you swatches so you can pick out your paint color and choice in carpeting as well as new furnishings. In the meantime, all the cabins on the property were equipped with stainless steel appliances, new plumbing and new HVAC systems."

"Wow, thank you. The house sounds pretty grand. Although I would be just as contented with the cabin. How thoughtful. I didn't expect that," Nancy said, with much enthusiasm.

Kelsey smiled. "Employee retention is important to me." Someone with Nancy's reputation and skillset would give her ranch credibility among the other ranches. "And selfishly, I'm hoping to give you impetus to start earlier than six weeks. The success of this ranch is important to me. I've got starter herds being delivered in a few days and I'm going to need your expertise."

"I understand." Nancy straightened. "Give me two weeks. Might be sooner, but I know I can be there in two weeks for sure."

"Perfect. That timeline works for me. I'll be in touch with the hiring papers."

Once they ended the video call, Kelsey puffed her chest and grinned at Trevor. "That went well."

"It sure did." Trevor laughed and held up his pen. "I'm taking notes for my own business because that compensation package was unreal." His eyes held such respect, which made her proud of the extra work she had done to prepare for her interviews.

Truth be told, Kelsey had felt a little foolish, *desperate* even, for going above and beyond, but her efforts had snagged her a great foreman. "Thanks. Each offer was tailor-made." She patted the papers on the table. "I had special incentives for the other applicants as well if they were chosen. Nancy said she was a single mother in her cover letter so I knew that she would need to consider her son when making a decision." Nodding, Trevor scribbled on his notepad. She tugged on his sleeve. "What are you doing?"

"I wasn't kidding when I said I was taking notes. I'm going to have my assistant offer individualized end-of-year bonuses—not just money—this year. I usually just give everyone the same check—and they will get that. But they will receive something extra moving forward. Personal." He tapped her nose. "You taught me that. You gained a new employee and her respect in one swoop. Well done."

Her cheeks warmed at his praise. "So, it wasn't too much?" She lowered her lashes.

"No. It was just right." Trevor cocked his head and used a finger to lift her chin until she faced him. "Don't be afraid to be you, Kelsey. I know I told you to be firm to get respect. But kindness goes a long way as well." He touched her face, his expression tender. "Frankly, your kindness is intoxicating."

"I did have ulterior motives though. A need that had to be met," she pointed out. "With you, I needed help on the ranch, and with Nancy, well, I need a good foreman."

"Don't do that," Trevor said gently, with a shake of his head. "Don't detract from what you've done from the heart because it is very much appreciated."

"Nope, I'm selfish and I'll prove it." She drew her chair close to his and slipped her hands around his neck. "Right now, I'm thinking only of myself. Of the pleasure you'll give me when you press your lips on mine. It's all about me," she teased.

Curving his body, his lips hovered above hers. "You're wrong again because we're both going to enjoy this immensely."

"You make me nervous," Kelsey confessed, dragging her teeth across her bottom lip. "But you also make me feel excited. I went to bed last night thinking about our kiss." Her pulse raced and she had shivers on the inside.

"Such conflicting emotions..." Trevor trailed kisses across her neck and chin. "I'm sure I can tip the scale toward excitement."

"Oh? How do you plan to do that?" she asked, her breath choppy as she tilted her head to give him access.

"I'd tell you, but I think you'll like it better if I *show* you." He crushed his lips on hers and showed her in exquisite, toe-curling detail. And she was there for it. All of it.

Chapter Five

When Trevor woke up the next morning on the king-size bed of the luxurious guest suite and stretched, his foggy brain was confused for a minute. *Where am I?* Then he scanned the oversize quarters with its private bath, which featured a Jacuzzi and two walk-in closets, and relaxed.

That's right, he and his children were at Kelsey's. There was a connecting door that led to a large sitting room, which was where they had settled the triplets for the night once the movers had arrived with his possessions.

Trevor asked his voice assistant for the time and shot up when he learned it was five thirty, thirty minutes past his usual waking time. He blamed it on the most decadent mattress and bedding he had slept on in a while. He planned to take a picture of the mattress and pillows for his place.

At this time of day, the triplets were still asleep, and he treasured these precious moments to reflect and plan his schedule. He quickly got dressed, minus footwear, and, grabbing the baby monitor, padded down the stairs. He had his work shoes near the door. Hearing movement in the kitchen, he headed that way and stopped short. Kelsey was also up and fully dressed, also barefoot. Her red hair was up in a bun, messy, sexy and flowing in all directions.

There were two cups of coffee, toasted bagels and a fruit salad on the island. "Good morning." He smiled. "That looks delicious."

"Thanks...it was no trouble. I always make myself a big breakfast. Working on the ranch builds up my appetite." She gave him a shy look before pointing at the spread. "Grab the plates. I'll get our coffee."

They settled outside, admiring the view of the sun coming up over the horizon. While they ate, Kelsey outlined her tasks on the ranch while Trevor gave a brief rundown of the daily routine that he tried to keep with the triplets. He wasn't always successful, but tomorrow was another day to try again, right?

As they spoke, their feet had their own conversation. It started with those soft, smooth toes rubbing against his under the table. She wasn't even aware of it, biting into her bagel and moving her toes. Trevor didn't move a muscle, enjoying the intimacy. The sheer randomness of it all. And the effects of those actions on his body. She was thrilling him without even trying. *This is so hot.*

The thought of leaving his children with Kelsey caused a pang in his chest, momentarily dampening his desire. "This might sound funny to you, but I'm already missing the triplets. I've gotten used to being there with them."

Her foot stilled. *No, no. Don't stop.* Kelsey gave his hand a quick squeeze. "No, it doesn't. I get it. I'm used to doing my morning chores on the ranch. Owning my ranch was a dream and I'm not going to put that to the side but I really want to help you out." She bit her bottom lip. "Like I said last night, we just need to coordinate our schedules so it works for both of us."

"I'm listening." Or trying to listen as she spoke, but she was driving him mad. Her toes moved up to his ankle.

Fighting a groan, he bit into his bagel. *Wait. Does she know what she's doing? Is she messing with my equilibrium on purpose?* His eyes narrowed as he studied her. Nope. She was focused on their conversation as he should be. He zoned in on the words coming out of her mouth and not her mouth itself.

"I was thinking that I would go by the ranch early every morning and get all my chores out the way, then when I get back, we can get the children fed together."

"That could work. And, I can move my company check-ins to the early afternoon, during their nap time."

"Yep. And then we can take care of the kids together in the evenings and during bedtime."

A glob of cream cheese hit her cheek. Trevor wiped it off with his thumb. A thumb he stuck into his mouth, causing her to stop mid-sentence, zoning in on said thumb.

She scooted close and demanded, "Next time use your lips," before plopping the last piece of fruit, a juicy pineapple, into her mouth.

"Will do." As if on cue, the juice trailed down the side of her face. Raising a brow, Trevor was only too happy to oblige.

He lapped up the liquid then crashed his mouth down on hers. The next beat their tongues became entangled in a duel of sorts, neither caving, neither backing down. Until the baby monitor crackled to life with a wail, tearing their mouths apart. Chest heaving, she excused herself to see about the babies, and after finishing his meal, he joined her. His heart expanded at the sight of his children giggling and jumping in their cribs. His children had slept as well as he had.

Sounds of *Dada, Daa, Dadadada*, delighted his ears.

Together, they got the children changed and dressed in matching onesies. Then it was feeding time. Happy babies meant bouncing babies which meant a lot of the food ended up in hands, faces and on the floor. He could hear the leaves of the trees fluttering in the wind. The weather app predicted heavy rains, so Trevor offered to get to the ranch and check on the sheep and cattle.

"Are you sure? I don't mind getting my hair wet."

"Absolutely sure. Besides, I want to see how the workers are doing. Jonathan said his people would be here for a week. Mine will remain until Nancy arrives and you've got people hired." He gave his children kisses on their foreheads. "I love the schedule you've come up with, but on my way out to your ranch, I called the nanny agency to see if we can get part-time help in the mornings and evenings. They carefully screen their staff, and they only employ the best but they should be sending over their top candidate. I'll be back in time to meet with her and to relieve you."

"Okay, that works. If I get a chance, I'll work on our blended schedule."

"Sounds good. See you in a couple hours." He gave her a sweet kiss and rushed out the door, jumping into his truck. What a great start to his day. But a call from his grandfather rang through the cab, threatening to ruin his buzz. Luckily, he knew how to fix that. "Boop." He hit the end button, sending the call to voicemail.

"You're a natural," her father said, coming to sit next to Kelsey on the couch. He had come home to drop off his laundry since this was one of the days they received housekeeping services, and she had filled him in on their temporary living companions. Since Sander had the left wing all to himself, Kelsey assured him that the Porters wouldn't be in his way.

But Dad waved her off, saying it was good to have little ones fill the house again. Then he went searching for his trail mix.

"Thanks, Dad." It was nap time, and William and Sasha had gone down on their own, tuckered out from playing. But James's tooth was still bothering him, so she decided to rock him until he faded out. Then she was going to catch some z's herself before heading over to the ranch. Taking care of babies was a never-ending cycle.

Dad popped some peanuts in his mouth. "Three babies are a lot for one person." He tapped her shoulder. "Even our family baby whisperer."

"I know. But I'll be fine. Trevor won't be much longer. In fact he texted that he was on his way, so he should be here any minute to interview the new nanny. How's your search for the family surprise going?" She patted James on the back, pinching her cheeks to keep from yawning. She didn't want her father to think she was overwhelmed, but goodness, she needed to rest.

"It's going... I'm planning on going to the boathouse

next week. You can come with me if you get things sorted out with your ranch and the children."

"I'd love to come."

Sander crooked his head toward the sleeping babies. "How long will you be helping Trevor out? I would think that he could afford to hire round-the-clock care."

"It's not that he can't afford it, Dad. It's that he hasn't found someone capable that he can trust. Like you were with me and my cousins, Trevor wants to be involved in his children's lives. His father usually helps him out but he's on a cruise until the end of the month. So, I won't be watching them for long." The yawn escaped. Now her eyes burned.

"All that's fine and good but what about your ranch? You've been talking about owning one for years so I'm concerned that helping with childcare is going to interfere with what you want to do."

"That's a fair concern. But this situation is mutually beneficial. Like now. Since it was pouring rain, Trevor decided to go tend to the ranch in my place. I'll be heading back over there once he returns."

"Still, it feels like he got the better end of the deal overall. You have a big heart and I'm proud of you to stepping in to help but I don't want you putting your dreams aside."

"Far from it. I will very much be involved with my ranch. I'll be alright, Dad. I promise." Of course, she had to yawn again. "In fact, Trevor contacted the agency and they are sending someone over starting today to assist."

James was now asleep. She gave him a kiss on the cheek before placing him with his siblings inside the playpen.

"Yeah, I get it." Sander scratched his chin. "Good help is hard to find. When is the sitter supposed to come? The day is half over already." The doorbell rang, and he gave her a lopsided grin. "It's like you planned it." Her dad chuckled and jumped up to answer the door. She heard a woman identify herself as the nanny. But it was the deep male voice that made her shoulders slump with relief. Trevor was back. Just like he had promised.

Kelsey really hoped this person worked out.

Her father and Trevor came in with a woman behind them. She appeared to be of mixed race, in her mid-thirties, and was dressed in a mousy brown shirt, pants and sneakers with her brown hair tucked in a bun at her nape.

"I'll leave you to it," Dad said. "I'll text you when I'm ready to go out to the boathouse."

"Thanks, Dad." She waved at him before giving the other woman a friendly smile.

But then she received a text from one of the ranch hands that wiped the smile off her face. It might be lambing time.

She jumped to her feet, energized. "I've got to get to the ranch."

"Yes," Trevor nodded. "I rushed back because I knew you would want to catch your first lamb being born on your ranch."

"I'm Amy Rossi," the woman said with a strong Italian accent, extending a hand, which had a surprisingly firm grip, and those eyes of hers were sharp. Trevor wondered if the outfit was a ruse, meant to fade Amy into the background. "I'm here to interview for the position."

Trevor ushered her into the living area to take a seat. "The children are down for a nap, and I can't wait for you to meet them. I'll keep this short since I need to get some shut-eye myself. Let's run through duties…" Afterward, he took Amy to introduce her to William, Sasha and James, making sure to let her know that James was breaking in a tooth. "He's been fussy but not as much today."

"Okay, does he have a pacifier? I can set it in the freezer to cool his gums."

"Oh, what a good idea! Although, I do have teething rings somewhere. I'll see if I find them."

"Yes, but I recommend the teething pacifier because most babies tend to keep those in their mouths. Sometimes, they use those round teething rings as ring tosses."

"You are so right." Trevor dug around the baby bag. "There are at least six in here." After a few seconds, she found one and handed it to Amy. Reaching for a teaspoon, the woman slipped both items into a ziplock bag and then placed it in the refrigerator.

Curious, he asked, "Why did you put a teaspoon in there?"

"That teaspoon comes in handy if one of the children bump their head and gets a knot. You press a cold spoon on it to help reduce the inflammation and swelling. Of course, it doesn't eliminate the need for professional care if needed."

Trevor emitted a loud yawn. "Fascinating." His cheeks warmed. "I'm sorry. This yawn has nothing to do with you. I've been going nonstop since this morning and it's catching up to me."

Amy cocked her head. "You look ready to fall off your feet. How about you go get some rest? I can clean up and sit with the children. We can talk more when you're feeling a little more revived."

The vision of his large, comfy bed was hard to resist. "Are you sure?"

"Yes." Amy pointed to the couch. "May I?"

"Oh yes. Absolutely. Sorry about that. You can leave your bag on the counter. Help yourself to anything you want in the kitchen, and you can put the television on if you'd like. We have every streaming app imaginable."

"Thanks. But I've got a book. I don't want to chance waking the children."

"That's right." Trevor chuckled.

"You're doing a marvelous job. Getting three children on a schedule takes finesse."

For some reason, that compliment made Trevor misty-eyed. Or maybe he was so exhausted that his emotions were all willy-nilly. "I appreciate your saying that." He walked toward the stairs. "I'll set my alarm for an hour, but I'll have my door open, so holler if you need me."

"Okay. See you in a bit."

Trevor made her way into his bedroom and slipped under the covers. He pulled up her phone and set the clock. Then he went online and ordered those teething pacifiers. There were some other cute items, but he was too tired to scroll through. It had to be seconds before he fell into a deep sleep. But the next thing she knew she was being shaken awake. It was Kelsey.

"Trevor, wake up. You've got to wake up. Your alarm was going off, but you didn't hear it."

"K-Kelsey? How did the lambing go?" She smelled fresh, like she had just taken a shower.

"Ugh. It was a false alarm. But that's not why I'm here." She clutched his chest.

He went on high alert and jumped to his feet. "Has something happened to the children?"

"You've got to see this." Kelsey held out a hand and they darted toward the stairs.

Heart pumping, he scuttled behind her, calling herself all kinds of names for leaving the triplets with a virtual stranger. He hadn't even spoken to the woman for more than five minutes. What kind of father did that make him? His feet couldn't move fast enough.

Suddenly, Kelsey stopped short, and he bumped into her, reaching an arm around her waist to steady her. Kelsey gripped onto his shirt. Her hair spilled out of her makeshift bun, settling all over her shoulders.

"Easy now," Trevor said, looking over head at his children. His mouth popped open. "William and James are walking! Whoa. They are *walking*!" He rubbed her eyes and took in the scene before him. Amy had cleaned up while he slept. She now stood in the kitchen, holding a dishrag, encouraging the boys to walk as well.

"Yeah, what are the odds that they would walk at the same time on the same day?" Kelsey said, amazed.

"I know right." He beckoned them forward. "Come to Daddy. Come on. Come on."

Of course, Sasha wasn't going to allow her brothers to outshine her, so she stepped past them and into his embrace. Then William turned toward Kelsey. She held out her arms for him. When his little body slammed into hers, Trevor's heart zinged with all kinds of feelings that he didn't quite know what to do with. Kelsey swung the baby around, making him laugh with glee.

Then Trevor and Kelsey traded children, clapping and cheering until they all ended up huddled on the floor. Sasha's foot was in her face and William and James were all twisted up on Trevor's leg. Although of course William had his foot in his mouth again. Trevor cracked up. He tapped his pocket for her phone, intending to take a picture, but he must have left it upstairs.

Kelsey seemed to read his mind because she retrieved her phone and took a few pictures of them.

Trevor stilled and locked eyes with hers. "You look beautiful," he whispered.

She touched Trevor's leg and whispered, "Later."

"I'll hold you to that."

Amy moved around them with a quiet grace, her bag on her shoulder. "I'm gonna head out unless you need something else. I wasn't sure what you planned to do for dinner, but I did make a fresh salad. The children finished the fruit salad."

"Oh no, you've done more than enough," Trevor said.

He stood and helped Kelsey to her feet. When their hands connected, an electric jolt raced through him. He had never been so aware of a woman in his life.

The babies toddled over to hug Amy's leg. For Trevor, that was a good sign. He couldn't keep the big grin off his face as he watched his children interact with their new sitter.

His eyes met hers and he came over to where she stood, then crooked his head in Amy's direction. "What do you think?" With a nod, she gave a thumbs-up, humbled that he had sought her opinion.

"Amy, how would you feel about working for us full-time?" Trevor asked.

The other woman smiled. "I would love that. Your children are absolute darlings."

"Wonderful. I'll have my admin, Graham Morris, draft a contract that we can review together tomorrow. Look out for an email from him." He winked at Kelsey. "I want to make sure you have a generous compensation package."

"That's thoughtful of you, Mr. Porter," Amy said. "But I—"

Trevor lifted a hand. "Please call me Trevor. We're pretty laid-back here."

Amy dipped her head. "By the way, I'm also available if you ever need round-the-clock care or need a weekend getaway."

"That's good to know." He shot Kelsey a lopsided grin. "We both will be involved with the children, but we might want a date night here and there."

Trevor gave a little laugh, but on the inside, he wondered, Didn't Amy have a family? A life outside her job? Trevor believed in work-life balance, and he didn't want to make snap judgments, but a carte blanche schedule like that made him wonder about Amy's priorities. Amy wasn't much older than they were. When would she date? Have fun? But then Trevor chastised herself. He hadn't been born with privilege and he had worked many double shifts to get where he was today. Maybe Amy needed to work and had obligations. Or she could just love her job and children.

By this time, William sat at Amy's feet, James encircled her leg and Sasha had her arms raised for Amy to pick her up. Trevor lifted his little girl in his arms and gave her a kiss on the cheek.

"I'll see you tomorrow, Mrs. Porter."

His mind raced back to their conversation earlier that day. He didn't remember saying he had a wife but Amy was through the door before he could correct that assumption.

Sasha kicked her legs before trying to eat his face.

"You're slobbering all over me, little girl," he said with a chuckle as he placed her with her brothers. He put one of their favorite shows on and headed back to Kelsey's side. He took in her wrinkled brows. "Is something wrong?"

"Did you hear what Amy said? You could have knocked me over with a piece of hay." Kelsey blew out a breath. "Amy thinks I'm your wife."

"Are you upset about it?"

She rubbed her arms. "No, not really, but it isn't the truth. She left before I could set her straight."

"I can see how she drew that conclusion," was all he had to say. What else could he say?

"I feel awkward talking about this. I'm not a wife or a mother. I'm not even in a serious relationship. So her words really caught me off guard. I'm not ready for anyone to place labels on me even though rationally, I understood why."

All Trevor could do was nod. "You seem to unphased by her comment. Am I making this a bigger deal that it needs to be?"

"Tomorrow, I'll let Amy know that you're helping me out and that we're just friends."

Just friends who kiss. And touch. And who have the hots for each other.

Kelsey changed the subject. "What are we going to have for dinner?" Her face flushed. "Gosh. We *do* sound like a married couple."

Trevor's arm went about her waist. He wasn't about to pick up that conversation thread. He wasn't ready to unpack all that. "How about pizza?"

"That sounds great." Her voice sounded shaky. She slipped out of his grasp and went over to stand by the playpen. "Who wants piiizzaaaaaa?"

"Pzzz," Sasha said, gripping the sides of the playpen to do a little dance.

"Dada." James tried to jump but he fell on his bottom.

William clapped his hands.

Trevor chuckled. "Pizza it is."

Kelsey went into the kitchen to call Donatello's Pizzeria. Trevor strolled over with his card in hand. But she shook her head. "I'm good."

"You are giving us free room and board. The least I can do is pay for our meal."

"I tell you what. When we go on our date, you can pay then."

He gave her a look. "We are together, correct?"

She nodded.

"We are going to share a meal, correct?"

She nodded again.

"Then it's still a date. We might have three little chaperones, but it is still a date. In case it's not evident, I don't allow just anyone to share my space with my children." He placed the card in her hand.

Kelsey sighed. "I see there's no point arguing... Do you want buffalo or barbecue wings?"

"Why choose?" he smiled.

So she ordered the pizza and wings.

When she ended the call, Trevor turned her to face him. "I didn't know I would secure someone permanent to help with my children so quickly. Do you have any second thoughts about our staying until month end? If you do, I can see if the rental is still available."

It was then Trevor realized that he didn't want to leave. Luckily Kelsey echoed his thoughts. "Despite my panic about being called your wife, I don't want you to leave. I would miss you and the children. I've grown quite attached to them in a short time." She squared her shoulders. "I want you to stay."

His stomach muscles relaxed. "It's nice to be wanted."

"You are." She moved into his space and smiled up at him. "It's later."

He frowned before understanding dawned. He drew her close. "Yes, it's later." He ran his hand through her red locks before peering into her eyes. "If I recall, I was telling you how beautiful you are. Inside and out."

She licked her lips. "And I remember getting all hot and bothered."

His eyes darkened. "Oh, how about I do something about that?"

Kelsey tilted her head back and challenged, "How about you stop talking and kiss me instead?"

Chapter Six

Good help was hard to find, but when you found it, it could change your life. Over the past week, Amy had been a godsend. Trevor would never admit it to his father, but she was a way better assistant than Pop was. Now to be fair, she was a professional. His children kept their set schedule and feeding time was a breeze. Okay, so maybe breeze was pushing it, but it was definitely more manageable.

However, though Amy was great, the best thing about this week had been getting to know Kelsey. Simply put, she was marvelous.

Love, a good heart, hard work. Values his mother had instilled in him, and Kelsey had each of those in abundance.

His triplets adored her. She treated the workers with such humanity that a couple of them had already told him that they were going to stay on to help Kelsey. Trevor hadn't been surprised or upset when he'd looked into those innocent green eyes of hers, assuring him that she hadn't tried to poach his crew. And she was hardworking.

That woman could outwork some of his best workers and was determined to keep going. Though Kelsey was rich and could put her feet up and let the crew work, she was right there with them, caring for the horses and working with the livestock.

Take for example, when the starter herds had been delivered two days prior. She had been right there with him to help with the inspections of the cattle, checking for strange bumps, rashes and snotty noses. Then she had meticulously reviewed their vaccination histories while his ranch hands assessed the bulls for reproductive quality.

For a man like Trevor, seeing Kelsey getting her hands dirty like that was downright intoxicating. His attraction for her had intensified. Every chance he had, he was tasting those plump lips. He couldn't get his fill. And she gave as good as she got, which drove him batty.

Now as Trevor stood in the mirror of the bathroom in his suite, early in the morning, brushing his hair, he tried to quell the jitters rolling around in his belly. Today, he planned to take Kelsey out on a real date, and his nerves were like jelly.

For one thing, he wasn't sure if she would think he was corny. She was an heiress and might expect that he would drive her up to Dallas and take her to the Talia 469, a swanky Michelin-starred eatery or maybe even to Lone Star Selects. But he wanted to share a part of himself—his interests—with her. Though Kelsey might not be down with that. She might think it wasn't cool enough.

He wasn't worried about connection. Or their ability to engage in stimulating conversation. But he *was* concerned about what she might think of his hobby. Because

Trevor was very much comfortable with who he was, but it would be nice to have a partner in his pursuits.

Well, there was only one way to find out. Amy was already on board to watch the triplets, and he had bought the tickets and signed them up for an event. He just had to get out of his head long enough to ask her. He decided he would ask her at the ranch. Once they were finished with feeding his children, they headed out to Fortune 8 to tend to the chores together.

It was a bright, sunny day which meant the ranchers were in good spirits as they bustled through the chores.

"Are you sure that this is a good idea?" Kelsey asked, holding the feed bucket overflowing enough to leave a trail of grain behind them, as they made their way to the sheep barn. One of the ranch hands had offered to carry it for her, but Kelsey had insisted.

Trevor nodded, carrying a bottle of apple cider vinegar and a couple boxes of baking soda in his hands. "Yes. Adding the vinegar to their water will keep it free of mosquitoes and algae. And the baking soda will help with their digestion. We'll mix it to their oats and barley."

"Okay, but if this doesn't work, I'm going to make you eat it."

Trevor chuckled. "I'd love to see you try."

Kelsey wagged a finger. "Don't dare me, Trevor Porter. I rise to every challenge I've been given in life."

Stopping at the entrance of the barn, Trevor admired her. "That you do."

Her face turned a rosy hue and she gave him a playful slap before sashaying past him into the barn. Once they were finished getting the sheep fed, Trevor and Kelsey followed the trail to the starter herds, which were now getting acclimated to their new home. The cattle had great temperament and seemed to be easing into their living situation without any aggression.

"They look happy," Kelsey observed. The cattle stood close together, grazing on the land, licking their noses and swishing their tails.

"I agree," Trevor said.

"Maizie seems especially happy too."

"Maizie? Should you be naming them? You don't want to get too attached."

"Yeah." She pointed to the scrawniest cow of the bunch. "She was a rescue. I plan for her to live out the rest of her days in peaceful tranquility."

"Okay. That sounds good." Trevor couldn't put off his request any longer. "Would you want to go out with me tonight?"

To his relief, her answer was swift. "Sure, I'd love to." She patted his back. "What time and how do I need to dress?"

"We'll go early afternoon. Dress casual. You'll need comfy shoes." Pity that those pretty toes—that were now a beautiful shade of turquoise—would have to be covered up.

"Got it." She did a little jig and gave him a quick peck. "I'm excited."

Oh boy. Doubt crept in. Trevor would hate to disappoint her. Maybe he should change his plans. No. Kelsey was down to earth, humble and gracious. All would be well.

Trevor reminded himself of that when they back at the

main house and he heard Kelsey talking to her father on the phone telling him she was going on a date. Sander had called asking if she could go to the boathouse. He didn't stick around to hear the rest of the conversation as he had to get dressed, but it sounded like she would meet up with her dad the next day.

Speaking of dads... Pop hadn't checked in as yet. Trevor had sent his daily good morning message with a picture of the triplets. Today their faces had been covered in Cocoa Krispies. Pop usually liked the picture or would send a GIF in response, but today there was nothing. Pop had said they would be docking in Barbuda, so he texted, Hope you're enjoying those pink sand beaches, before jumping into the shower.

After he was dressed, he checked once more to see if his father had responded. But nothing. The lack of a response was no surprise though. After all, Pop *was* on a romantic cruise with his fiancée.

Heading to the long mirror on the back of the door, Trevor turned this way and that, examining his black jeans, long-sleeved waffle shirt and cowboy hat. That would do. Satisfied, he headed out the door and went downstairs to wait on Kelsey. Based on past experience, it might be a while.

However, a mere five minutes later, she came down the stairs wearing wide-legged jeans and a geometric abstract art sweatshirt. She had her hair loose, and those glorious curls popped along with her glossy lips.

"Are you ready to go?" she asked. As if he hadn't been waiting there first.

He slipped his arm in hers. "Yes, we're not going far. We have a twenty-minute ride."

Amy was upstairs giving the children a bath, so he sent a text that they were leaving. On the ride there, he put on some jazz music in the background.

"Thanks for helping with the starter herds. I plan to—"

Trevor placed a hand on her lips. "No business talk. This is a date."

Puckering her lips, she kissed his finger. "Got it. So what do you want to talk about?"

"I don't know. Tell me something meaningful to you that you don't talk about often."

She lifted her shoulders. "I miss my mother. It might seem odd to miss someone you don't know. As I mentioned, she died when I was a baby. But I wish I knew what her voice sounded like." Swallowing hard, she confided, "My dad has shared pictures, but I just want to know if I sound like her or if she had a high-pitched voice or was it low and sweet... Sometimes, I cry about it. Even now."

Her admission touched his heart. "Didn't your father have any old videos?"

"Sadly, no. He wasn't married to Lani Harlow when she had me. She didn't want any permanent commitment. So, I don't know how many videos he had, but whatever he had were destroyed in a mini fire. He had them all in one place and they got destroyed."

Trevor's heart went out to her. He had videos of Claudia and pictures that he hadn't looked at in years. He would make sure to have them secure for his children. Every child deserved to know both their parents.

"I didn't mean to bring down the mood," Kelsey said softly.

"No, you didn't. I was just thinking about Claudia…"

"Yeah, I notice you don't talk about her much with the children."

"Well, they're nine months. I don't expect that they would understand anything I share right now. But at least they have each other."

"I guess I get your logic, but I hope you plan to let them know her." Trevor made a mental note to start talking about her more. He had been so focused on his tempestuous relationship that he hadn't considered that his children would one day crave even the smallest detail about their mother.

Kelsey continued talking. "I would have been so lonely if it weren't for my cousins. I'm glad my father took over their care after my aunt and uncle died. It was a lot, and Dad was just a year younger than me when his parents passed away, so for years I had no idea how he managed with such a great responsibility of rearing four children." She scoffed. "But he did and we're so close. Especially me and Priscilla."

Because he had been listening keenly, Trevor asked, "What did you mean you *had* no idea?"

"You caught that?" She looked out the window. "Your babies changed my perspective. In no time at all, they have a special place in my heart, but that makes caring for them natural. Now, there's a learning curve, a much greater one than opening a ranch, but it makes me understand my father's actions. The heart can make room for people we love. And it hurts me to know your babies will face the same pain I have one day. Unfortunately, there's no avoiding it." Her breath hitched. "The pain of never knowing a mother's love." He pulled into the parking spot and put the car in Park, silently processing her words. She dabbed at her eyes. "Sorry, I know you probably didn't mean for me to go that deep."

"Please don't apologize." He reached over to enfold her in his arms. "I'm honored that you trust me enough to share what is in your heart."

"Your devotion to your children touches me. You remind me so much of my dad." She caressed his cheek. "Your love will be a balm for their pain."

Oh, this woman was something else. Trevor gave her a gentle kiss. And then another. Kelsey was a willing participant. With effort, he tore his lips away. "If we don't get out of this car now, I'm going to try to make love to you in the back seat like a teenager."

"Then let's get out of here." Trevor put the car in Reverse, but Kelsey tapped his arm. "No, silly. I meant get out of the car for our date."

His face warmed. "Oh yeah. I knew that." He put the gear back into Park and got out of the vehicle before going around to open the passenger door. A warm, sensual floral scent hit his nostrils. "What is that fragrance?" he groaned.

"It's Valentino." She pursed her lips. "And there's a dash of it in some secret places."

Trevor's mouth went dry. "Secret places?"

She winked. "We can play hide-and-seek later."

"Hide-and-seek?" He swallowed. Beads of sweat lined his brow.

"Stop repeating after me." She crooked her head. "Let's go."

If she didn't know better, she would think Trevor was nervous to take her inside the Emerald Ridge Botanical Gardens. She had no idea why because this was one of her favorite places.

Before she purchased the ranch, Kelsey visited the gardens at least once a week, so she knew the layout well of the sixty-six-acre property.

He handed over their tickets for entry. Once admitted, she followed Trevor along the path and gasped. There was a table for two in the center of the gardens. The greens and the lilies with baby's breath lining the runner were stunning. After a meal of prime rib, twice-baked potatoes and grilled asparagus, Trevor took her on a tour of the specialty gardens, the conservatory and the boardwalk.

They strolled through the koi-filled ponds, oohing and aahing over the intricate stonework and waterfalls. Then they arrived at the rose garden, one of her favorite spots. There had to be close to two hundred varieties of roses. She inhaled. The fragrances were not just lovely, they were soothing, calming.

"This is beautiful. Breathtaking, really."

Trevor was looking at her, like the hero of a movie looking at the heroine. She could almost recite verbatim what he was about to say. With a soft smile, he bent over to whisper in her ear. "I agree."

Gosh, how many times had she called that corny when she saw it play out on screen? But, now that it had happened to her, she was blushing like a schoolgirl. "Thank you," she breathed out, feeling every bit as beautiful as he claimed.

With the beautiful colors of dusk as a backdrop, Trevor took her picture before he kissed her until she got all weak in the knees. Hand in hand, they went to the education room. There were three other couples present. There were different potted plants on display and numerous art supplies like fabric, string and paper spread across the table.

"Oh, we're making collagraphs," she exclaimed, rubbing her hands.

"You've done this before?"

"Just once. I was no good at it. You?"

His lips quirked. "I've done it once or twice. But I'm looking forward to making something with you." With the art instructor's assistance, they created a pattern together that was…passable. Not worth displaying, but it was all about the experience.

In the midst of their art making, Amy sent a picture of the triplets. They were dressed in matching yellow onesies and all three were standing up with happy smiles on their faces. "Oh, they are so cute. I could just eat them up," Kelsey gushed.

"Sometimes when they are sleeping, I stand there and watch them and I wonder, how did I get so blessed to be chosen as their father?" he admitted gruffly. "They are everything to me."

"Aww. I love how expressive you are with your feelings."

Trevor's phone buzzed. This time when he looked at his phone he frowned before slipping it in his pocket. "Are you ready for dessert?" he asked her.

This was the second time she had been in his presence when that happened. Once again, she was curious to know what that was about, but she didn't want to ruin their evening by asking.

"Yes, I'd love that."

While enjoying their tiramisu and ice cream at a cozy table for two in the restaurant, she noticed Trevor grew pensive. The conversation halted, and she finished her ice cream feeling uncomfortable. She just had to ask, "Trevor, what's wrong? You're tense."

He shook his head. "Am I? I apologize. I don't mean to be and it's nothing. Well, it's something but not the right topic for a date." Standing up, he took her hand. "It's time for our final activity."

Swallowing her retort, Kelsey followed him down the trail. He was plainly bothered by something and didn't want to open up to her. That hurt, especially since she had bared her heart to him earlier. Maybe he didn't view her as someone he could trust. She hated feeling as if these building emotions were all one-sided on her part. That this was just attraction for him.

But was she ready if he wanted more? Until she knew the answer to that, maybe she shouldn't press.

Now she grew quiet. She needed to think. Usually, when she had something on her mind, she would head to the bird conservatory... She stopped short when she realized that's exactly where Trevor had taken her.

"How did you know?" she asked, amazed.

There was no way Kelsey Fortune, a woman of considerable wealth and substance, was a bird watcher.

It has to be the most boring hobby in the world. Who just sits around looking at Aves? Claudia had tossed those words, mocking him when he had invited her to sit with him, which was why he had been apprehensive about bringing Kelsey here. All he had sought was tolerance, but she had been thrilled.

After emitting a loud squeal, she had dragged him to the gift shop to buy two binoculars, and they picked out T-shirts for the triplets. Now she sat next to him on a bench, rattling off facts, like there were over three hundred species here in the gardens, and pointing a bunch of them out.

"My favorite though are the hummingbirds. The ruby-throated to be precise," she said, peering into her binoculars.

"I'm an owl man myself."

"An *owl*? They are so spooky with those large eyes. And they are hard to spot, such masters of camouflage."

He couldn't resist taking another picture. She was just so cute with the binoculars pressed to her face. She waved a finger toward the trees. "Oh, I think I spotted a grackle. Did you see it? Man, I wish I had my camera. I used to post my findings on eBook. Do you do that?"

"No. But I used to keep a notebook with sketches."

"Really? I'd love to see it if you still have it."

"I don't have them anymore." He cleared his throat. "I haven't done this in about a year, actually, since I've been trying to figure out fatherhood, but I plan to get back into it."

"Makes sense. The triplets are high priority."

Trevor looked at his watch. "Speaking of which, we'd better get back if we want to catch them before bedtime."

"Yes, but we've got to do this again. And of course, we'll bring the kids when they are a little older."

The fact that Kelsey was planning events for the future told Trevor that she was thinking long-term. That knowledge made him smile.

On the way back to the car he asked, "How did you even get into bird-watching? You're the first person I personally know that has this for a hobby besides me."

"I got into it because I love nature, and with a house of six there were times I wanted to get away and think."

"Same. Except I also just loved the research. Do you have other hobbies besides this one…?"

They continued small talk during the drive back to the ranch. He parked in his usual spot and turned toward her. "Sorry to see our date come to an end. But before we go in, I just want you to know that I had a great time today."

"I did as well." She bopped the bridge of his nose. "But who said this is the end?"

Chapter Seven

Kelsey tested her toe in the warm bath, enjoying the scent of jasmine with a dash of eucalyptus. She added more hot water until it was just right. Sinking in the tub, she rested her head against her bath pillow and closed her eyes. The heat on her back felt so good. Her muscles were thanking her right now.

The knowledge that a few feet down the hall Trevor was also in the shower tantalized her senses. Water flowing over those strong shoulders, his tight abs, that firm butt—ah, boy, she couldn't wait to hold on to that. The thing is, Trevor had no idea how fine he was. Seeing those muscles protest against his shirt as he tossed bales of hay like they were a bag of feathers, as the sweat poured down his face, was a major turn-on.

And tonight, he would be hers.

Once they had gotten the kids down, she had asked Trevor to give her an hour before coming to her suite. She stayed in the tub until the water cooled and her skin wrinkled. Then she wrapped herself in a large towel and padded out of the bathroom. She pulled open her drawer and took out a hunter-green bodysuit lingerie and put it on. When she saw it in the catalog, she'd hit the buy button without thinking. Kelsey twirled in the mirror. She had to admit she looked hot, but the material was way too constricting.

She had to fight to get it off her body. Returning to her drawer, she chose a red flannel short pajama set with lace trimming instead. Yes, this was more to her liking. Sexy yet comfy. Kelsey then sprayed the Valentino perfume in strategic places.

There was a soft rap on the door.

When she opened it, she saw Trevor's broad, bare chest. Her eyes trailed to the pajama pants hanging low on his hips. Dang. She had to shut her mouth to keep from drooling. He held a baby monitor in his hand, which somehow didn't detract from his overall coolness. She snatched him close to her and closed the door.

Trevor hoisted her in his arms in one swift movement and trailed kisses along her collarbone. "You said something about hide-and-seek?"

She opened her mouth to respond, but he planted his mouth on hers. Her arms spread around his back, and she held on. She heard a deep intake of breath before he moaned, "You smell so damn good," followed by deeper kisses. He placed her at the edge of the bed and took her top off. Those deep brown eyes zoned onto her breasts. She folded her arms.

"They are too small. Not my best assets."

"Beautiful," he breathed out as his hands cupped them. "They are the perfect size."

Kelsey had planned a fun bird trivia challenge, where the loser gets undressed, but Trevor's hands were already slipping her shorts off her legs as he continued his "thorough investigation." She closed her eyes, moaning as his mouth explored her body, uttering, "Found a spot." That reminded her of a trivia question. "Trevor, which bird had the longest tongue?" she huffed out.

"Hmm?" She repeated the question. "The northern flicker." He then did the most marvelous thing with his tongue. She gripped the sheets.

Her breath became choppy, and she struggled to think of another question, but her thoughts had fizzled like this trivia game. But even through her pleasurable haze, she registered that he was doing all the giving.

Well, she couldn't have that.

Tapping on his shoulders, she scooted back on the bed and crooked her finger at him. He climbed onto the bed and raised a brow. "Am I doing something wrong?"

"No. But this needs to be fun for both of us." She commanded him to lie down, undressed him and then proceeded to love on his body. A give-and-take ensued. Their passion building, sheets twisting, steady climbing until they crashed into oblivion, entangled in each other's arms.

Within minutes, Trevor was asleep. Kelsey though didn't settle right away. That was the best night of lovemaking she had ever had. Because it was more than two people finding physical release. It was deeper. And it left her troubled. Trevor came with heavy baggage in the form of three nine-month-olds. Nine-month-olds who needed a mother. Kelsey wasn't the person to fill that slot.

She hadn't even had a mother growing up. She might be good with other folks' kids, but she had no example of how to be a mother.

And that scared her.

There was a faint cry coming through the baby monitor. If she didn't go, it would be followed by an even louder, longer cry.

Slipping out of bed, she went into the nursery. It appeared as if all three babies were asleep. With the nightlight as a guide, Kelsey sauntered over to the cribs to check on each child. Though Kelsey and Trevor had put them in on their backs, Sasha and James had rolled onto their sides. William was burrowed into the corner of the crib. There were bumpers, but she moved him back onto his back in the middle of the bed.

Looking down at them, her heart tugged. The poor darlings should have a mother. Could she fill that need? That question made her stomach tighten. Stepping backward, she spun around and left the room. She crept back into bed and nestled into Trevor's back. *What the heck am I even thinking?* Being a mother to triplets required a large shoe size, and her feet were a tad too small.

"Mornin'. Ready to find a treasure?" Dad asked as soon as Kelsey walked up to the boathouse. He had on jeans and a light jacket and held two Starbucks flasks, which made her smile. She'd had to drag herself from under Trevor's arms this morning.

They both had slept in until the triplets woke up, and Kelsey blamed their lethargy on Trevor waking her up in the wee hours for a round two and then a two and a half. A half because she'd had to plead that she couldn't take any more of the onslaught, squirming and begging for mercy.

Trevor had chuckled, kissed her lips and promised, "To be continued."

She could hardly wait to make him beg in turn.

But for now, there was coffee. A large cup of roasted goodness to perk her up and warm her insides. She reached for the cup. "Hey, Dad." Normally Kelsey would greet her father with a kiss on the cheek, but when she remembered her exploits the night before and where her lips had been, he got a hug. Oh, yeah, that would have to do.

Along with her brown checkered flannel shirt and matching jeans, she had slapped a pair of Dolce & Gabbana shades on her face, and it wasn't just to shield her eyes from the sun. It was another set of discerning eyes she was worried about.

Kelsey gulped down some of her coffee and pointed toward the sleek building, which featured a rooftop patio with glass railings, outdoor showers and two boat lifts. There was a lot of possible hiding places. "Off we go." They walked up the ramp and stepped onto the deck. Memories of her and her cousins racing around the wrap-around deck, hurling themselves across the sun loungers, diving off the springboard, or simply gathering for a light meal around the outdoor dining table in the corner of the deck brought a smile to her face.

Her father placed a hand on her back. "We had a lot of good times here."

"Yeah, we sure did. I can still hear you yelling at us to quit running on the deck before we slipped and hurt ourselves."

Dad laughed and took a sip of his coffee. "Every time we came here, I would lose my voice." He shook his head. "You all were such a handful, I wondered what I was thinking when I agreed to be the guardian of four grieving children. I tell you that was a labor of love."

Kelsey eyed the horizon, picturing the three babies she had come to care about. "If you had to do it again, would you do it? Meaning do you have regrets of what you should have done with your life if you hadn't been saddled with so many kids?"

"None. Not a one. And, yes, I would absolutely make the same decision again. I'm so proud of how the each of you turned out. A father couldn't ask for anything more. As far as I'm concerned, taking care of my brother's children—and you—was my destiny."

He said that with such certainty that it lifted her spirits. "Thanks, Dad." Finishing off their coffees, they rested the cups on the outside deck and began their search. For the next few minutes, they thoroughly searched the exterior of the deck until they met up again by the springboard.

"Do you remember when Roth thought he was an Olympic swimmer and tried to somersault, but his foot got caught on the board?" she asked.

"That boy." Dad shook his head. "He hit the water wrong and fractured his leg. I was so afraid that day."

"You were?" she asked with surprise. "You didn't show it. You dived after him when Roth sunk under the water, and to me, you were my real-life superman." She leaned into him. "You're still my hero."

"I didn't do anything. That's what a father does."

Kelsey thought of Trevor. She could see him doing the very same thing for his children. He wouldn't hesitate to help one of his children in need. "Dad, I think I've developed feelings for Trevor."

Sander tensed up beside her and stepped back. "We're getting distracted from our search. We should go have a look inside." He stomped off ahead and inputted the four-digit code to unlock the door.

Okay... She hadn't expected him to be joyful, but she didn't think he would shut down on her. Kelsey was too much of a daddy's girl to drop the discussion. "Dad, I need to talk about this."

"We have a lot of area to cover."

He opened the shutters to let in the natural light from the large windows in the open living space. The kitchen had been renovated with top-of-the-line appliances, and the dining area accommodated up to eight people. She looked further around the room. The leather sectional in the living room was resistant to cracks and fading so it almost was the same as when her father had purchased it years ago, especially since he kept it covered when not in use.

Inside was a bit nippy. She wrapped her arms about herself. "Are you really tuning me out right now?"

"I need a minute to think. To recalibrate. This wasn't what I had in mind for you." Her father turned on the heating. "It should warm up in a minute."

"Okay, I get that. Truth be told, I'm in processing mode myself."

"Let's start in the bedrooms upstairs and then work our way down."

"Alright."

They bounded up the stairs and started in the smallest room, then the other two bedrooms, the master and bathrooms. Not finding anything, Kelsey and her dad returned to the first floor.

She wanted to respect her father's request, but she did have a question. Were they processing the same issue? "Dad, when you say this isn't what you had in mind, were you talking about his race, or…?"

His head snapped toward her. "You should know me better than that. We have a blended family that keeps growing. This has nothing to do with race, although, you know that's a challenge in itself for anyone who dates outside their race. I'm talking about the fact that you've never had a serious relationship. Just short, safe flings. You've never had your heart broken or fallen in love—not that I want you to have your heart broken—but you were focused on other things like riding and now ranching." He sighed heavily, scrubbing a hand over his jaw. "And now here you go, jumping feetfirst into a ready-made family, which comes with lots of sacrifices and responsibility."

"You don't think I'm ready for it?" she asked in a small voice as they started their search. It was then she realized she wondered the same thing and was seeking her father's assurance. Sander wandered into the kitchen while she looked in the dining room.

Kelsey bent over to examine under the table. She raised her volume so her dad could hear. "Trevor is a widower, and he's got three babies—not one. Three. I've grown attached to those babies already, and I just don't want to make a mistake." She moved to search the chairs' upholstery for zippers or hidden linings. "I don't want to hurt Trevor and the children, but what if a few months from now or a few years from now I feel differently?" Her voice hitched. "And, what if I let this go because I'm afraid then I never find this again?"

Dusting off her hands, she wiped her brow with her elbow. There were only cobwebs. So far, the only thing she had discovered is that the boathouse could use a good cleaning. She went to wash her hands in the powder room then went into the living area.

"And where does Trevor fit into this equation?" Dad asked, coming out of the kitchen to join her. He took the covering off the couches, and they pulled the sectional apart to inspect every nook and cranny. "You said you care for the children, but when they're grown and gone, you'll be left with the man."

"I honestly have no clue…" She slapped her forehead. "This is way too hard."

Dad chuckled. "Don't I know it."

"Great." She sighed. "Now I'm more confused than ever." By this time, she had worked up an appetite. "I'm hungry."

"We'll grab breakfast at the diner when we're done." Kelsey glanced at her watch. Amy and Trevor were probably feeding the triplets now. She wished she were there to help them.

Her dad came over to hug her then leaned against the partition separating the living area and the powder room. "Sweetie, you're thinking too hard. You're strong and capable and your heart is big enough for all of them. But you're searching for a guarantee, and life doesn't work that way. I don't know if we're ever ready for anything. There's only one thing we can do."

"What's that?" She moved closer to him, resting her shoulder against the wall.

"You've got to let your heart lead the way. That's all you need to know when it comes to readiness. Now, with that being said, I've never known you to back down from anything just because it was tough. You're indomitable and you persevere. That's who you've always been."

"Thanks, Dad."

"No thanks necessary." He tucked her under the chin. "The way I see it? That man knows a good thing when he sees it. I don't blame him for latching on to you. But you don't have to figure this all out today, sweetie. Allow yourself to live in the moment and just enjoy it." He lifted off the wall. There was a small snapping sound.

They both frowned. "What was that?" she asked.

Her father tapped and tapped then pressed his ear to the wall. "It's hollow."

Excitement built in her chest. "Do you think we've found it?" *Oh my goodness.* Was this surprise actually real? Dad lifted a finger. Then he reached up to the top of the wall and tore off the thin strip of wallpaper.

"This is a different color than the rest. It's a false door," he shot out, reaching up to pull on the partition. Kelsey rushed to help. "After three let's pull. One. Two. Three!"

The wall came down.

They stepped back so they could see.

"It's a secret door," she squealed. "Do you think the surprise is in there? Should we try to bust the door down?

Or do you think there's a key hidden somewhere?" She spun around and her eyes narrowed, searching the space to see if any clue would present itself.

Her father felt around. "It's metal and I don't see any way in." He pumped his fists. "This has to be it. This has to be the door."

"I can't believe we've actually found a door! This is unreal. After all these years of searching, we might have *finally* uncovered Mark and Marlene's surprise!" She clapped her hands.

"Yep. And there has to be a key somewhere." He straightened, his voice filled with resolve. "Now all we have to do is find it."

Chapter Eight

"If you're up to it, I'd like to show you my home. They finished the plumbing, and the electricity is up and running," Trevor said to Kelsey as they exited the drive-in theater. "Now it's time for me to pick out cabinetry, patterns and paint swatches, and I'd love to get your thoughts."

Kelsey had returned from the boathouse that afternoon on a high. She had talked in detail about her family's hunt for some hidden treasure, and they had finally had a breakthrough. Though Trevor hadn't quite followed everything, her excitement was palpable, and he offered to take her out to celebrate. She wanted to include the children.

So he had given Amy a paid night off and they had bundled the kids in their car seats and gone to see *Zootopia*. The Emerald Ridge Drive-In featured older movies, and for five dollars, a family could enjoy a film on the big screen on the field. The triplets were too young to understand all that was going on, but they could dance along to the catchy tunes in the movie.

"Sure, I'd love to," she said, munching from a huge tub of popcorn. Her lips were greasy from the butter, and he so badly wanted to have a taste of that salty goodness. But since they had made love, besides a few light kisses, he had backed off a bit. He hadn't expected their union to be such an assault to his equilibrium. Instead of pacifying his attraction as he thought, his body now craved her. At night he burned, wanting to knock on her door, but somehow, he'd found the willpower to refrain.

Besides, it wasn't like she had come knocking either. So, maybe she too was having some second thoughts. He didn't think she had regrets, but she *was* keeping her distance. Kelsey tossed some popcorn in her mouth and gave him a smile.

"You're really enjoying that," he said once they stopped at a traffic signal.

She flashed him a mischievous grin. "When I like something, I go all in."

His groin registered those words. "I'm a witness." Kelsey was a generous lover. When Kelsey beckoned to him and took charge, Trevor went with the flow enjoying every minute of her loving on him.

Now he wanted more. And that scared him.

"We're here." He inputted the passcode to open the gates. Kelsey leaned forward to peer into the dark. "I'm going to install some solar lamps to line the driveway." He proceeded up the path and stopped in front of the regal home.

There were two large pillars on each side of the steps leading to the front door. When he looked back, his children had fallen asleep. "I'll leave the car running, and we'll have a quick look-see." He turned on the interior lights.

"Do you think they'll be alright?" Kelsey asked worriedly.

"Yes. This is private property and there aren't any neighbors around for miles." Then he added, "I don't want to wake them because then we'll have fussy babies to deal with tonight."

"Okay, but can we crack the windows at least? It'll make me feel better."

"I would, but I don't want any bugs getting inside here. But I've got it covered." For someone who had never been a parent, Kelsey sure acted like one. Her concern for his children made him like her even more. Trevor asked Kelsey to FaceTime him. Answering his phone, he placed it on the dash, so he had a clear vision of the back seat.

"Oh, that's smart." Kelsey was all smiles, the relief evident in her tone.

She got out of the vehicle, and they dashed to the front door. Then he took her on a quick tour of the upper floor since that was finished. Each of the five bedrooms on that floor had their own private baths and walk-in closets. She loved his bedroom the most. "We're going to have a lot of fun in here," he couldn't resist saying. They returned downstairs.

"The rooms are so spacious, and I like how each room has a theme, and the family room in the loft area looks inviting," she declared, her boots clicking on the hardwood floors. "The nursery and playroom are simply divine. And I love that you have pictures of their mother up. She's stunning."

"Thanks. Sasha is Claudia's imprint. It will be a while

before they'll have their own bedrooms, but I wanted to make sure they'll have enough space to spread out."

"Wow. You've thought of everything." She cocked her head. "It doesn't sound like you need me at all."

Trevor grabbed the books and swatches. "I do need a woman's touch, and I value your opinion." He wanted to say he needed *her* touch, but he didn't want to have Kelsey think he was putting any claims on her.

They headed out the door and back to the vehicle. Kelsey ended the video call, and he began the trek back to her house. They worked together to put the children into their cribs. Then they crept out into the hallway to talk. She tilted her head to look up at him, her eyes like dark emeralds in the light. "You have a lovely home, Trevor. Thank you for the tour."

"You're the only person who has seen it." He ached to run his fingers through her luscious coils.

She straightened. "Really?"

Trevor touched her cheek briefly. "Yes, Kelsey. I'm particular about who I let into my private domain. You're special to me. I hope you know that."

"I do now." He eyed her plump lips. "And I feel the same about you. I'm picky about who I open up to."

"Our night together was one for the record books."

"I know. But... I have some concerns." She dipped her chin to her chest. He heard a note of uncertainty in her voice and hated that he put it there.

A light knot formed in his gut. "What kind of concerns?"

"Well, for one, I feel you're guarded. Closed off somehow."

"Why do you say that?" he asked thickly.

"I opened up to you and told you about my mother. Something I don't talk about much, if ever. Yet you haven't done the same."

"What do you want to know? I don't have anything to hide, so if I've been closed off as you say, it wasn't intentional." By tacit agreement, they walked toward his bedroom. She sat on the large lounge chair. After placing the books and swatches on the nightstand, Trevor perched on the edge of the bed, unzipped his hoodie and slipped out of his jeans. Then he donned a pair of shorts and a sleep shirt, grabbing one for her.

"I don't know." She lifted her shoulders. "I just want to be sure that whatever this is between us, that it isn't one-sided." She looked down at her clothes. "I should run and change."

"No need. I got you." Walking over to where she sat, he took off her pants and cardigan set before slipping the shirt over her head.

"This feels really soft," she murmured. "You might never get it back."

"It looks better on you anyway." Trevor joined her on the armchair, with her sitting between his legs, her head resting on his chest. They shared a kiss, then, cupping his hands over hers, he began, "My mother died of ovarian cancer when I was eighteen years old, and it was on her deathbed that I learned my true identity. I learned that my mother, Samira Porter, was actually one of three illegitimate children of Hammond Porter of the Porter Oil billionaires. He'd had an affair while conducting business in India."

Her head popped up and she flipped over so she was on her tummy facing him, her eyes wide. "Your grandfather is Hammond Porter? How did I not make that connection?"

Trevor flattened his lips. "Unfortunately, I have no control of my heritage, and I have absolutely nothing to do with that man." He didn't even try to withhold his bitterness. Kelsey opened her mouth like she was about to interject, but he placed a hand on her lips. "I'll explain.

"My mother and her two siblings lived in India, and Hammond supported them though he didn't claim them. Told everyone that Phillip was his only child. Anyway, all was fine until my mom fell in love with a blue-collar guy. My Pop, Orson Holmes. When she married my father, Hammond cut her off. But then she got pregnant with me and Hammond gave Orson a big payout." He blew out a ragged breath. "Mom was furious when she found out. She saw it as Hammond trying to control her. Pop said he did it to secure their future, but Mom was so upset she left my dad and changed both our names back to Porter."

Kelsey placed a hand on his chest. "Oh, I'm so sorry to hear this, Trevor. Did your mom and grandfather ever make peace?"

"No. I don't think they ever spoke again. Mom told me that love, a good heart and hard work are what mattered. Those were the values I held dear to my heart when I sought to build my empire. They helped me become successful in my own right. I have no need for Hammond Porter or his money."

"If your mother was here, she would be proud of your accomplishments," she said softly.

His chest constricted. "William is a blend of both me and my mother. I'm glad to know her heritage lives on through us. I just wish my mom were here to see her grandchildren grow up."

"Yes, family is important." Kelsey kissed his chest.

"I agree. That's why I searched for my father, and we've been close ever since."

She locked eyes with him. "Your grandfather is also your blood. What about giving him a chance?"

"Nope. He snubbed my mother. I stood by her hospital bed as she took her last breath, and because of Hammond Porter, she didn't have her siblings by her side. He cut her off, but now *I've* cut him off."

She squinted. "Is he the one that has been texting you?"

"Yes." He grunted. "He keeps apologizing and trying to insert himself into my life. When all I want is for him to leave me alone."

"Wow." Kelsey's face fell. She pushed herself upward. "You don't sound like the man I've been getting to know. The man I care about."

Her disappointment weighed heavy on his chest. "What's that supposed to mean?"

"I thought you valued family."

"He isn't family. I don't know that man."

"When we hurt, we sometimes seek someone to blame, to pin all our pain on. Your grandfather sounds like he regrets his actions and wants a relationship with you. Doesn't he deserve a chance to get to know you and his great-grandchildren?"

"He deserves *nothing*." Trevor jumped to his feet. "This is where we have to disagree."

Kelsey also stood and gave a jerky nod. "The thing about unforgiveness is that it festers. It controls us. And it leaves behind nothing but destruction and hurt. You don't want any of that pouring into your children, the way your mother poured that into you."

Fury raged through him like hot lava as he tried to unpack that truth bomb. "My mother loved me."

Kelsey walked to the door and pulled it open. "I don't doubt that for a minute. But love doesn't shield you from making mistakes." She leaned into the doorjamb and folded her arms. "Answer this. Why did your mother tell you about Hammond Porter? She could have taken that knowledge with her to the grave, and you would be none the wiser. So did she tell you to hurt you, or did she hope for something more?"

Darn her wayward tongue. After their discussion the night before, Kelsey half expected that Trevor would pack up his family and leave.

But he was still here. When she popped into the kitchen that morning, he was already there, fully dressed, and, if her nose was right, making pancakes for breakfast. Sure enough, the telltale ingredients were all on display. Flour, eggshells and drops of milk littered the countertop. Kelsey received a grumpy, "Good morning," and a strong cup of coffee.

"You're up early." She took a sip before adding cream and sugar.

"Yes, well, I didn't sleep last night." He slapped a couple of pancakes onto a plate.

She hadn't either. Because she knew Trevor was put out with her, she hadn't closed her eyes for more than an hour or two. So, when the sun came up, her eyes were wide open. The positive was that she'd caught a beautiful sunrise with the birds chirping outside her window.

"I'm sorry if I upset you. I meant well." She rested her coffee mug by one of the place mats.

"*Meant well?* By talking bad about my mother?"

Is that what she had done? Kelsey replayed her words and grimaced. "Oh goodness. I've made a mess of things. That wasn't my intention. I only wanted you to consider that maybe your mother wanted you to make peace with your grandfather through you." She tossed the eggshells into the trash can and put away the other ingredients.

"Make peace?" he sputtered, flipping the pancake with precision.

"Because facing death has a way of changing one's perspective." Kelsey washed a dishrag in warm water and wiped down the countertops.

Trevor shrugged. "Well, I'm not changing my mind when it comes to Hammond Porter."

Kelsey rubbed his back. "You lost your mother, but Hammond lost a daughter too. You're a father, Trevor. I imagine that must be a parent's worst nightmare. Having their child go before them."

He paused midair, spatula in hand, before he shook

his head. "No. I don't think Hammond cared. He didn't even come to the funeral."

Making eye contact, Kelsey asked gently, "Would you have welcomed him there if he had?" Trevor couldn't quite meet her eyes.

He dropped the pancake on the platter and grunted. "I don't know... Can we stop talking about him right now? Please?"

Hearing his agitation, Kelsey realized she had pushed enough. Trevor would have to come to certain realizations himself. She had planted the seeds and would let the matter rest. At least for now. That's when she noticed the splashes of pancake batter on the stove, dripping from the bowl. Mr. Porter was a messy cook. An adorable messy cook. And he looked especially cute with her apron around his waist. Why hadn't she noticed that he was wearing that before?

"Your pancakes look delicious, and they smell heavenly."

He gave a half smile. "This was my mom's recipe. This might sound odd, but whenever I miss her, I cook something she taught me. It makes me feel closer to her."

"Oh, it doesn't sound odd at all. It's touching." She'd never had that. And neither would the triplets, which saddened her. They ate their pancakes outside on the patio, enjoying the quiet before the kids woke up and Amy arrived.

Trevor ran upstairs to get the books and swatches, and together they picked out paint colors, art and other decor for the kitchen and dining areas. Trevor's enthusiasm was infectious, and he planned every aspect of his house with meticulous detail, evident by how much time they spent poring over eggshell versus flat paint. But she'd had fun because she was doing this with him.

One day some lucky woman was going to walk into that house and gasp. Trevor had thought of everything.

A cardinal landed on the hedge near to them. "Look at that," she said, snapping a photo.

"She's a beauty." He looked over at Kelsey. "You know they say that cardinals represent a loved one who passed away. I'd like to think my mom paid me a visit today."

"Aww. I like that. I thought they represented the power of a strong family. Stability."

"It can be both," Trevor said quietly.

They joined hands and smiled. Gathering their plates, they went inside to load the dishwasher. Trevor washed the pan and wiped down the stovetop. It was nice to see he didn't mind cleaning up his messes.

"My new ranch foreman should be driving up today," she said. "Nancy sent me an email early this morning confirming her arrival. So when we get to the ranch, I'll help with the chores, but then I'm going to hop over and make sure Nancy's cabin is ready for her. Then I'm meeting up with my cousins at The Style Lounge. Can you hold down the fort for me at the ranch?"

"Yep. And don't worry about the chores. My workers and I will take care of them for you." He wiped his hands with a paper towel. "Will you be getting your hair done?"

"Yeah... I'm getting highlights, a mani-pedi and a full body massage." Kelsey snapped her fingers. "And I almost forgot. Our family gets together once a month to have dinner. I think we're meeting at Francesca's Bar and Grill for lunch this time. You're welcome to come with the triplets if you'd like."

"No. I don't want to intrude on your family time. We're not family."

Then why were they beginning to feel like that to her? The truth was, she had grown so close to Trevor and the triplets that she really couldn't see going to the dinner without them. "Okay, but if you change your mind, it's an open invitation…" She would have to text the family group chat to see the date and time. "Do you have plans for Thanksgiving? It's a little more than two weeks away."

"Nothing besides getting the triplets matching turkey outfits."

She chuckled. "You love to dress them in matching outfits."

"I guess I do, and I plan to do so until they stop me. But I should be moved into my home by then, and we'll be celebrating our first Thanksgiving as a family in my new home."

Without her. Another blatant reminder that she wasn't family. She wasn't permanent in his life. Just in it for a reason and a season. But did she want a lifetime?

"My family generally has a huge gathering on this complex. It's open to everyone and anyone. My dad has it catered. There is every kind of meat and dessert imaginable. And we play a contentious game of football." Talking about that cheered her up.

"Sounds like you all have a good time."

"Once again…open invite."

"Thanks." Trevor glanced at his phone and frowned.

"Something wrong?" she asked, thinking that his grandfather might have texted and warning herself to stay out of it.

"No. Well, yes. I haven't heard from my pop in a few days. We were texting daily before." He shrugged. "But he's on a cruise with his fiancée. Maybe he's busy enjoying his woman and texting me back isn't a priority." He sighed. "You think I'm just being a worrywart?"

She exhaled, glad this wasn't about his grandfather. "No, you're just concerned, but like you said, he's probably okay." Trevor was such a thoughtful man. She could fall for him if she wasn't careful. Although she suspected that she was already halfway there.

Chapter Nine

We'd love to have you for Thanksgiving if you haven't made plans, his cousin Jonathan texted just as he was finished with the morning chores at the ranch.

His second invite today.

Trevor considered that a blessing. But he really wanted to spend his first Thanksgiving in his new home with his children and father. He could see the large spread of turkey, pot roast, mashed potatoes, green beans, mac and cheese and cornbread on his long, mahogany dining room table.

Truthfully, his vision now included Kelsey, but as she said, she would be with her family and their significant others, which didn't include him.

Maybe he should accept Jonathan's invitation though. It would be good to see Jonathan and Imani and to catch up, but then Hammond might be there. He doted on Phillip's children and was bound to make an appearance. Trevor didn't want to have Hammond all up in his face trying to make small talk, as if *I'm sorry* fixed anything. Naw, it was best he stay away because Trevor didn't want to cause a scene by telling that man all about himself. He fired off a response to Jonathan.

Thanks for thinking of me but I am spending Thanksgiving here in Emerald Ridge. He added a smiling emoji since it was easy to misinterpret the tone you meant to convey. But his cousin didn't fully buy it, judging by his response.

Okay, fam. FYI, I don't think my grandfather is coming if that changes anything.

Dang, was his opposition to Hammond's presence that evident to everyone? And how was he supposed to respond to Jonathan's text message?

Kelsey's question came back to him. *So did she tell you to hurt you, or did she hope for something more?* He had been pondering that since she asked. Why did his mother tell him about Hammond and the Porters? Surely, it wasn't because she hoped for reconciliation? Trevor remembered how she struggled to speak but had pushed to tell him the truth about her past.

Just then one of his workers ran over to where he stood. "Hey, boss. We have a problem with a couple of the starter herd."

"What's going on?" They hurried toward the shed. "They've been lethargic and off feed. We were about to milk them when we saw their udders were red and swollen."

"That sounds like mastitis." If it was the case, then they had to separate the cows quickly since it was contagious. Trevor broke into a jog then. "Have everyone halt the milking, disinfect all the teats, and I'll call the vet." He sent Kelsey a text to alert her about the cows and then rushed inside to help.

The vet, Kelsey and the new foreman, Nancy, all arrived at the same time. It took a couple of hours before they had a treatment plan in place. The veterinarian started the cattle on antibiotics, and Trevor and the men would rotate their watch over the few days until the cows were better.

"Thank you, Trevor, for your quick thinking today. The vet said if we had waited, it would be worse," Kelsey said as they walked toward the parking lot. Nancy had already left to finish moving into the cabin. Kelsey had ordered a bouquet to welcome her new foreman to the ranch, and just learned that it had been delivered. They were going to both drive home, Kelsey would grab the flowers, then she would drive back to make sure Nancy was settled. The woman's son wasn't coming until after Thanksgiving, so Kelsey invited Nancy to dine with her family.

Trevor overheard their conversation and that made him think of his faithful, wonderful nanny. He hadn't seen or heard Amy talk to or about family. She seemed to be a private person who kept her work life and personal life separate, and he wasn't about to pry. However, as soon as he got home, Trevor planned to extend an invitation for Amy to spend Thanksgiving with him.

"Mastitis spreads really quickly, but if we follow all the vet's directions, they will be good as new." He looked down at her freshly painted toes done in a beautiful shade of blue. "Are you going back to the salon? I feel bad now for interrupting your beauty regimen."

"I'm glad you called. This is my ranch and this is my responsibility." She waved a hand. "And, as for my hair appointment, that's the least of my worries. I'll get it rescheduled."

"If it's any consolation, I think you're beautiful. Whatever you do, it's just enhancements on an already perfect package."

Kelsey blushed and gave him a playful shove. "Okay, where were you in my teenage years? You're going to be an awesome girl dad."

"I'm just stating facts." He drew her close. "Now give me a taste of those lips. I've missed you." They kissed long and deep until they heard cackles and whistles from the workers milling about. Quickly, they jumped apart, and he noticed Kelsey's face was flushed. Trevor was glad his melanin hid his embarrassment, 'cause, yeah, that kiss was hot. "I forgot where I was for a second."

Kelsey gave him a playful pinch. "Later."

He tipped his hat and winked at her. "I'm going to hold you to that. Do you need me to help with the bouquet?"

"No, I've got it." She spun around, giving him a view of her juicy derriere in those Levi's jeans.

Trevor cupped his mouth and hollered. "Girl, I'm jealous of those jeans 'cause they hugging you real tight right now." He could hear a few snickers behind him.

"Stop." She giggled. "You don't even talk like that on the norm."

He wiped his brow and waggled his brows. "It's your fault. You hypnotizing me."

Kelsey snorted. "You are hilarious, Trevor Porter." She got into her truck, slipped on her boots and blew him a kiss. "See you at home."

Home. Home was fast becoming where Kelsey was. And wherever she was, was where he wanted to be.

Trevor darted to his truck and caught up with Kelsey just as they passed the wrought iron gates. Then he hit the gas. The cool thing about driving on private property was that there was no speed limit. He rolled down his window and howled. She raised her fist in the air and revved her truck. They sped down the path side by side, her mane flowing in the wind. They pulled in front, tires squealing in protest.

Laughing, they jumped out of their cars, and she jumped into his arms. "That was exhilarating. I haven't driven with such abandon since I was a teen."

"Me either. It felt good to let loose." Trevor gripped her butt and kissed her hard before placing her to stand. Her lips were reddened from his kiss. Desire shot through his veins and his breath quickened. "Later?"

She nodded eagerly. "Later." Then she gripped his shirt and gave him a kiss that made him want to hoist her on the back of the truck and take her in the open air. Releasing him, she held his hand. "Ready to head inside?"

"I'll be in a minute. I just need to cool down."

"Good idea. My dad's inside."

His mouth dropped. "*What?* Why didn't you tell me?"

"Would you have kissed me the way you did if you knew?"

"No."

"That's why." And with a mischievous grin, Kelsey whipped her hair, *yes, whipped her hair*, and strutted into the house before leaving with the flowers.

When he got a hold of her tonight, he was going to

make her scream. Lord knows when he left in a couple weeks, he was going to miss that woman.

Why does it have to be goodbye? Why not a hello to new beginnings?

Trevor's cell buzzed with a notification from the Emerald Ridge Encores that his electronic tickets were available for download. Yes! He was going to give his administrative assistant a bonus. He didn't know how Graham had done it because they had limited seating, and all showings had been sold out. Trevor couldn't wait to see Kelsey's face when she learned he was taking her to see *Mamma Mia!* Graham had even managed to secure VIP seating plus a cast meet and greet.

He sent Graham a text. Thanks, my man. Give yourself a bonus.

Graham fired back. You're welcome. And I already did. Trevor smirked. Graham took efficiency to a whole other level.

Another text message pinged this phone. This time it was his Pop. Hi son. I think I'm okay now. He *thinks* he's okay, now? Trevor's brows furrowed. What did that mean? A series of likes from Pop on the pictures he had sent of the triplets followed.

Pop, are you alright?

Yes. We'll talk once I'm back. Give my grandbabies a kiss from their Pop Pop.

Trevor put a thumbs-up emoji on the last text. He should feel relieved that he had finally heard from his Pop, but all these messages did was raise another concern. What wasn't his father telling him? As he stepped into the foyer and three little people charged toward him, Trevor tried to focus on the positive, but his father's elusive text had served to replace one worry with another. Something was going on with his father and it caused a niggle of unease in his gut. And not even Kelsey's enthusiastic response to his surprise distracted from his fear.

"I'm so glad you changed your mind about coming with me," Kelsey said to Trevor as they followed the server carrying two high chairs to the reserved area marked Fortunes at Francesca's Bar and Grill. Kelsey held James while Trevor toted Sasha and William.

"It's all this talk of surprises and murder that's got me intrigued." After they had made love, Kelsey and Trevor had engaged in some serious pillow talk around her aunt and uncle's hidden surprise and Linc Banning's murder investigation.

Though Linc's murder had made the Emerald Ridge paper, Trevor hadn't paid much attention to it. Now, however, he was fully invested in learning the outcomes of both. Besides, spending time with Kelsey, meeting her family and hearing anything the family had to say about either of those topics were added bonuses.

Kelsey chose the two seats on the end. The server placed the high chairs in the space next to them, before going to get a third one.

When she texted the group chat to let them know she was bringing a plus-one with three, there had been much speculation about whether she was next to get hitched or engaged. She had shut that down quick, stating that she and Trevor were just friends.

That half-truth made her cheeks warm.

They were definitely more than friends. The things they did to each other last night should be declared illegal. But they hadn't committed to being in a relationship. Not that either of them was seeing anyone else.

They didn't bed-hop.

Kelsey and Trevor worked together to straddle Sasha and James into the high chairs. William, the most laid-back of the three, sat patiently in her lap. He pulled on her hair. As long as he didn't tug too hard, she was okay. Sasha and James were now banging on the chairs and making each other laugh.

"Are you sure it's alright that we brought them?" Trevor said. "Amy was more than willing to watch them."

"Yes, it's totally fine. They will blend right in with the other children. You'll see."

Roth and Antonia were the first to arrive along with her one-year-old daughter, Georgie. Kelsey stood, giving them each a hug, and introduced Trevor. The two men shook hands, and she was glad that Roth sat next to Trevor and started chatting it up with him. As the eldest, Roth was fiercely protective of Kelsey and his sisters.

The server brought out a high chair and placed Georgie next to Sasha and James. Soon the three children were egging each other on and having a grand time.

Harris and Sofia came in with her six year old daughter, Kaitlin and seven year old son, Jackson, as well as Zara and Sander in tow. After another round of kisses and hugs, they settled on the side of the table with Harris facing Trevor. Then finally Priscilla and Jax walked up with baby Liam in his car seat. They sat him between them.

Trevor leaned over to her and whispered, "I feel much better now that my kids aren't the only ones making noise."

"I told you. My family loves babies, as you can see, and that started with my dad opening his heart to my four cousins to raise them. And let me tell you, Roth gave him a hard time when he was a teen, but I digress. As I was saying, Roth, Harris and Priscilla are all with partners who have children. They each have interesting stories. But I'll save that for another time."

Trevor looked around. "There are a lot more children here than I thought there would be."

A couple servers came to take their orders, which included everything from burgers to salad to salmon and steak.

"Francesca's is only one of the top family restaurants in town. They are family owned and their aesthetic is family, friends and food."

"I love that." Trevor relaxed and reached for her hand under the table. "By the way, I'm glad I came. Your family are cool people."

"Thanks. I think so too."

Trevor's cell buzzed. He narrowed his eyes before swiping the message away and placing his phone face down on the table.

Instead of asking him about it, Kelsey focused on the hum of voices around the table. Everyone laughed and joked together, pulling Trevor into their conversations.

He blended in well with her family, talking and acting as if he knew them for years instead of minutes.

Her dad, who had chosen to sit close to the children, seemed to be having a grand time playing with the babies. And they were eating every moment up. Kelsey loved that, snapping a few pictures. She recorded a few short videos to watch later.

Their food orders came in. Kelsey and Trevor stood, intending to move the high chairs, but her father, Zara and Antonia waved them off.

"Your father is so laid-back," Trevor said, cutting a piece of his broiled salmon, which he had paired with a strawberry salad.

"He's the best ever. Honestly, every Fortune at this table turned out to be decent, hardworking human beings because of him." The fish had a golden brown seared top that gave Kelsey food envy. Suddenly, her loaded baked potato and tomato bisque wasn't as appealing, but she took a sip of her soup anyway.

"I believe it." He sounded wistful. "I found my father less than a year ago, and his presence in my life has been impactful. He is such a great grandfather that I wonder what my life would have been like if I had Pop around when I was young. Not that I didn't appreciate my mom. She was my world. But I'm glad my children are getting what I didn't have in a male role model."

She felt a pinch of sadness. "I applaud you for building your circle."

"Thanks. There are days where I'm more scared of being a father than of running an empire like Porter Cuts, but they are worth it."

Right as he said that, Sasha rubbed her hand full of mac and cheese all over Sander's cheeks. Kelsey jumped to her feet, but her dad waved her off. "I can handle a little gunk on the face." She returned to her seat, groaning at the stain on Zara's blouse. That orange color wasn't coming out anytime soon.

"Did I say that your family is wonderful?"

She smiled. "I wouldn't change them for the world." She eyed his salmon again.

Trevor sliced a good portion of his salmon and put it on her plate. "Have some."

"No. No. I couldn't possibly eat this. I have more than enough." She attempted to move her plate away.

"You've been eyeing it ever since the server put it in front of me. I want you to have it." His longer arm reach enabled him to put the fish on her dish.

"Okay, but at least let me give you a piece of my potato."

He grinned and made room on his plate. "I thought you'd never offer."

As lunch progressed, Kelsey and Trevor came out of their bubble to once again converse with the rest of the table party. Eventually the conversation shifted to Finn Morrison's adoption file.

"I've been waiting for this." Trevor scooted his chair closer to the table. "So, what exactly happened there? Kelsey explained, but I still don't quite get this whole adoption scandal and how it ties in with Linc Banning's murder."

Priscilla wiped her mouth and chimed in. "I know it's a little convoluted but I can try to explain. Apparently,

Linc Banning approached Finn Morrison to sell him his adoption file and Finn agreed. But then Linc backs out, telling Finn that he didn't have his file after all, and the next thing you know, he winds up dead. That's when I learned that Linc had left his houseboat to me. We also learned that he was approaching adoptees and attempting to make a profit by making them buy their birth records."

"Really? This guy sounds like a piece of work. How did he even get hold of those files?" Trevor asked.

"I don't know, honestly," Priscilla said. "But when I went to clean out the houseboat, I found the files hidden in the lift bed."

Trevor's mouth popped open. "This is fascinating. I'm sorry, I know that someone lost their life, but this is intrigue on a whole other level."

"We're still trying to piece it all together. But we believe there is a connection between Linc and Finn. We can speculate but we don't have any solid reasons as yet," Roth said.

"But we're not giving up our search," Dad added. "We're going to figure this out, layer by layer, until we uncover the truth."

"Yes, everyone deserves to have their truth told. No matter how unsettling it makes you feel," Trevor agreed, his eyes on his food.

Kelsey had a feeling that Trevor was thinking about someone other than Finn. Someone like his mother who had upended his world while she was on her deathbed.

Chapter Ten

When Kelsey pulled up to Walsh's Equestrian Estate a couple days later, she smiled at the fond memories of summers spent here riding.

This beautiful sunny day was a perfect day for it too. But that would come, especially if she found the horse she was looking for. She'd gotten a tip that a Camarillo White Horse had arrived from California, and she was here to preempt the auction by offering a generous price.

Luckily, she knew the owner, so she had an edge. If all went well, she would be leaving with the horse in the horse wagon hitched to her ride. "Hey, Aaron," she called out to the tall, wiry man barreling toward her. He appeared to be in a hurry, but she was determined to snag that horse.

"Kelsey. I heard you were coming. She's a beauty," he tossed over his shoulder. "As you can imagine, I've had several offers. Why don't you go have a look-see at Carmelina and then we can talk?"

"Wait," she called out and scuttled over to him. "I know she's in high demand. But did you review *my* offer?"

He rocked back on his heels. "Not yet. I had to go to

the police station, so I didn't have a chance to look at it as yet."

"Oh, that's right. I heard you were going down there. How did everything go?"

"Well, there isn't much to tell. I saw Linc Banning arguing with someone just weeks before he was killed, and with the investigation dragging on, I thought it prudent to let law enforcement know." He slapped his thigh. "It may or may not be useful, but I'll leave that for them to decide."

"Every bit of info will help their case. Have you heard anything more? Like are the police even close to finding the killer?"

"They didn't say. Not that I didn't ask, mind you. But all they did was politely thanked me and sent me on my way. Said they couldn't discuss an ongoing investigation."

"I get why they would say that." she said, somewhat deflated. "This is such a mystery. I have no idea who would want Linc dead." A shiver ran up her spine.

Aaron spat on the floor. "I'm hopeful that justice will be served. Now, I didn't know Linc personally, but like you said, he was close to all you Fortunes growing up." He gave her a penetrating stare. "What I did hear was that there were some kind of adoption papers found on Linc's houseboat. The police think that those papers are what got him killed. What's that about?"

Kelsey stepped back. "I don't know but this is just… sordid. Feels personal somehow."

"Seems maybe you didn't know him as well as you thought."

"Seems so. I adored Linc as a kid, and I just can't see him mixed up in anything like trying to sell adoptees information about their true births."

Aaron sized her up before finally nodding. Kelsey released a breath she didn't know she was holding. She heard a horse whinny and chuckled once she realized that it was Aaron's text message notification. He seemed nervous, jumpy. "I've got to go. One of my mares is in labor. But I trust you. If you want that horse, she's yours." He tapped the edge of his cowboy hat and took off for his vehicle. "Have a good ride."

Kelsey figured Aaron would be going in the opposite direction, but the horse pushed that out of her mind. She gave a celebratory whoop. Then she called Trevor. "I got it. I got the horse! They are hitching her up now."

"Oh, Kelsey, I'm happy for you. I can't wait to see her. A horse like that is a rare breed."

"Thanks." She ran her hand through her tresses. "How are the cows doing?"

"They are much better. I just checked on them. You'll see for yourself when you get here."

"Cool. What a relief." She placed the phone closer to her ear. "I have a couple more stops to make but I should make it back in time for the interviews."

"Alright. Drive carefully."

She ended the call and began her drive downtown. Nancy had chosen a dozen applicants, four of them being women. Kelsey covered her face with her hands, daring to hope. If these workers panned out, she would finally have a fully staffed ranch. Excitement bubbled within. Things were finally looking up for her. With Thanksgiving twelve days away, she was going to have a lot to be thankful for.

Kelsey made it back to the ranch in good time. Nancy rushed over and whistled. "How did you manage to snag one of these?"

She grinned. "Small town benefits. I know the owner. Aaron Walsh."

Nancy froze. "Did you say Aaron Walsh?"

"Yeah, do you know him?"

"I knew an Aaron Walsh once but no way that's him…"

Kelsey waited for the other woman to elaborate, but Nancy didn't volunteer any more information. She didn't want to meddle by peppering her with questions. The women unhitched the trailer and then led the horse to the new stable. Carmelina would have exclusive quarters and plenty of space to graze and exercise.

"You have enough land to make a gallop track," Nancy observed. "You can even make a path through the woods to give you even more riding land."

"You read my mind. I'm going to fence this area, bank the corners and install sand footing. Then I'll add a trail through the woods, but I've got to get the rocks cleared out first." She blew out a plume of air. "There's a lot to do."

Her foreman nodded. "I'll develop a plan of action for you and provide you with an estimate of how much it will cost."

"Thank you. I'd really appreciate that. I forget that I don't need to do this on my own anymore."

"Certainly. Right now, I'm studying your books and

your current processes to see how we can improve efficiency and eventually start making you some money."

"I've no doubt that with you in charge, my cattle ranch will be quite profitable."

After talking shop, Kelsey searched for Trevor. Maybe she could steal a couple kisses before heading downtown. Not spotting him, she sent him a text and learned that he had gone home to help with feeding the children. Kelsey still had her errand to run downtown, so she swallowed her disappointment as she headed to the dress boutique. She needed something elegant to wear to the musical. Kelsey knew that there hadn't been any seats left when she had checked, so she was thrilled that Trevor had somehow managed to snag a pair of tickets.

Kelsey darted into the store and in twenty minutes she was dashing down the block, dress in hand, into The Style Lounge. The owner of the upscale salon, Sofia Gomez Simon, tapped her watch, shaking her head.

"I made it. I made it." When Kelsey called that morning, Sofia had said she could fit her in if she made it there before 2:00 p.m.

"With two minutes to spare." Sofia directed her to an empty chair. Then the transformation began.

Thirty minutes before closing, Trevor paced outside The Style Lounge. He should not have put this off. If he hadn't, he would have driven to Dallas to get a shape-up, but time slipped away from him.

Why hadn't he checked to see if there was a black barber in town? he berated himself. Since moving here, Trevor either had his father cut his hair or he had driven to Dallas or to the next town over. The door chimed and a couple of people came outside. One was a white guy. He had a low cut, and the fade wasn't too bad.

"My man, did you get your hair cut in there?" he asked.

"No, I just came to get my girl. I got this done over on the other side of town."

"Alright, thanks." Trevor walked up to the window and peered inside. He locked eyes with one of the stylists and backed up. *Daggonit.* Maybe she hadn't seen him.

No such luck. The woman came to the door. "Can I help you?" She was edgy cool, dressed in all black, her hair cut asymmetrically, shaved on one side and dyed pink. And her lips and nails were black.

He stuffed his hands in the pocket of his jeans. "I, uh, wanted to get a haircut, but I don't know…"

She opened the door wider. "Sure, come on in. I can tighten you up."

He bit his lip. She sounded so confident, but if she jacked him up, it would be weeks before he could fix it. And he'd have his workers ragging on him. Maybe they would post his picture on social media, and he would be a laughingstock.

"You coming?" she asked, raising a brow.

His chest heaved and his palms were sweaty. If there was a sister in there, he would feel better. Trevor scratched his head. He wanted to look his best for Kelsey. Maybe he could try again himself. Trevor was good at giving himself a fade; it was when he had to line up the front that he ran into trouble. He tended to go way past his hairline.

"Well? We are about to close." She chuckled. "I got you. I promise. It will be alright."

He touched his beard. "Okay, let's do it." Tamping down his trepidation, he stepped inside the door and sat in the chair.

Forty minutes later, Trevor stepped out, with a huge grin on his face and a little extra swagger in his steps. The young woman, who went by Dodge, had serious skills, a new customer and enough bills to keep her smiling until his next visit.

Standing at the bottom of the staircase later that night, Trevor had to close his mouth to keep from drooling. He made a show of fanning himself as Kelsey came down the stairs. "Somebody call 9-1-1 because it's smoking in here."

She stopped before him and giggled. "More like we need to call the corny police."

Trevor laughed before giving her a light kiss. "You're a vision." Her hair had been straightened with highlights of brown and gold flowing on her shoulders. She wore a form-fitting red sequined dress with a thigh-high split, providing him a great view of those long, shapely legs. But the scene stealer was those strappy stilettoes with her new pedicure on full display.

"You look pretty sharp yourself."

He touched his fade and ran his hands across his black tailored dress suit. "This old thing."

They grinned at each other. Trevor stole another kiss then pulled away. "Let's get out of here before I try to take you on these stairs."

Her green eyes darkened and she sat on the steps, giving him a come-hither look and arching her brows. "I would be amenable to being taken here."

"Quit playing, girl."

In one swoop, Kelsey stood and strutted into the kitchen. Then she swung her hair and gave him a sultry gaze. "I'm about to get some dessert for the road. Care to join me?" she breathed out. *Oh, she is putting the sexy voice on. Alrighty.*

"We don't want to be late," he warned, even as his feet had a mind of their own. Trevor strolled into the darkened kitchen to see Kelsey in front of the open refrigerator with a slice of three-layer chocolate cake in hand and a knife in the other. Amy was upstairs with the children, so he knew they had the kitchen all to themselves. He took the knife and placed it on the countertop. Kelsey used her finger to scoop a piece of the sumptuous cake and put it in her mouth.

"Hmm. Delicious."

This woman was playing games when they needed to get on the road. But hey, he could get with that. They could spare a few minutes. Trevor mopped his brow and took a step closer. "Let me get a taste of that."

She leaned forward and puckered her lips.

"I meant the cake," he said, stone-faced.

Kelsey gave him a playful shove and laughed. "Whatever."

"I never joke about cake."

Using her finger, she picked up another glob and placed it in his mouth. Trevor licked it off her finger. Her breath caught. His hands spanned her waist, and he drew her close. She gasped from the evidence of his desire. Slowly, he lowered his head and kissed her, her scent driving him crazy. Between the heat of his tongue and the coolness of the refrigerator, Trevor knew her senses had to be on high alert.

Then he dropped to his knees. Leaning in, he kissed her inner thigh, intending to work his way up, when the lights came on. He froze. The brightness startled him. He looked upward to see horror written on Kelsey's face.

There was a loud gasp from Kelsey and a "What the—" from her father.

Sander. Her father. Kelsey's dad.

"D-Dad, wh-what are you doing here?" she stuttered out, her nails biting into his shoulders.

"I live here," Sander said.

Lord, open the earth and swallow me now. Trevor did the only thing he could think of and that was to make a show of buckling her shoes. Then he stood facing Kelsey and practically yelled, "There, your shoes are all fixed."

"Her shoes, huh." Sander didn't sound like he was buying that excuse. But there was no way Trevor was turning around. "I was coming to get a piece of cake, but I see you two beat me to it," he said.

There was an edge mixed with amusement in his voice. For sure, Kelsey's dad knew what they had been up to, and the older man was enjoying making him squirm. Trevor knew this because if this had been his baby girl, he would do the same thing or worse. Not that he wanted to think about Sasha doing anything like this. *Ever.*

Trevor went to the refrigerator and grabbed the cake. With the island as a shield, he placed the chocolate confection on the countertop and cut a slice. Kelsey skittered over to the cabinet. There was a lot of clinking and nervous chatter before she returned with a plate. She placed the slice on the dish and handed it to her dad. All this was from his peripheral because Trevor couldn't look Kelsey's dad in the eyes. In this moment, he had no idea when he would be able to ever again.

"There's nothing like having your cake and eating it too," Sander snorted, after taking a bite. "But I'm sure you know that." Whoa. Talk about a mic drop. Kelsey's dad then did the slow walk out of the room, laughing to himself, disappearing around the bend.

"That was mortifying," Kelsey moaned, slumping against him.

"Yeah, tell me about it. I lost a year of my life just now," Trevor said, moving away from her and to the other side of the room. "From now on, I'm keeping my distance when we are anywhere other than the bedroom."

Kelsey cracked up. "It will be fine."

"Easy for you to say. Your father didn't catch you on your knees."

She reached out her hand. "Let's get going. We don't want to be late."

He ignored her hand. "Oh, *now* you're concerned?" he mumbled, turning off the kitchen lights.

"Wait, grab the rest of the cake."

"Nope. I think we have both had enough. Don't you agree?"

"How about we finish it later?" she whispered, slipping her fingers through his.

He must have a serious problem because Trevor was

tempted. "Maybe," he said begrudgingly, before guiding her out to his mustard yellow Aston Martin and opening the passenger door. He had stopped at his house to trade out his truck for this one.

"Boys and their toys," Kelsey teased, getting inside, once again giving him ample view of her legs. Trevor averted his eyes. Those legs had just gotten him caught on his knees. Literally.

"I know you're not talking. I saw Carmelina prancing around on the ranch."

She giggled. "I have a Ferrari in the garage too."

"I hear you. We work hard, so let's play hard," Trevor said before he gave her a lopsided grin. "Put your seat belt on, sweetheart, 'cause you're going to need it."

Chapter Eleven

Trevor wasn't taking any more chances. After a wonderful experience at the theater, he suggested they finish out their night at his place. He had to stop there to return his car and get his truck, so why not stay until the morning?

That way there would be no interruptions and that room was already furnished. He could make love to Kelsey all night long, and make her scream until she was hoarse, and no one would hear but him.

"But what if one of the babies get up?" Kelsey asked, drumming her fingers on the door. "They are used to having us there. Have you been apart from them before?"

"No, I haven't. But I trust Amy and I'm not that far if there is an emergency. Not that there will be."

"I don't know…" She dragged out the last word, her anxiety triggering his.

"Okay, how about this? Let's call and check on them. Then decide."

"Yes, I like that idea."

Trevor put his cell phone on the center of the dashboard and made the video call. There was a text message from Graham, but he would call his assistant back in the morning.

Amy answered immediately. "Hello, how was the theater?" She was in the nursery and there was a night-light on, but behind her all was still.

Kelsey leaned over. "Oh, it was marvelous. I was singing at the top of my lungs." She jabbed Trevor in the ribs. "So, was he. Well, he was trying to, but he didn't know the words."

"Yeah, but at least I can carry a tune. The people in the row before us begged Kelsey to stop singing." He snickered. "At one point, they offered to pay her if she would shut up."

"Whatever. I had fun."

Amy cracked up and turned the camera, but the room was darkened. "The children went to bed at eight and they haven't even stirred since."

"That's good to hear." Kelsey relaxed into the seat.

"Okay, if all is well, we'll be back no later than five tomorrow morning." His tone sounded normal, but he was doing somersaults on the inside.

"That sounds good." Amy waved and Trevor ended the call.

As soon as the line disconnected, Trevor was out the door and running to open the door for Kelsey. Excitement was a drum beating in his chest. He was going to share his new king-size bed with Kelsey. Something he had dreamed of since getting to know her. Hopefully, it would be many more to come because he couldn't picture anyone else that he wanted in his private space. In his bed. Or in his heart.

Trevor had suspected for a while that he had strong feelings for Kelsey, but he admittedly hadn't done a lot of soul-searching about it. However, for the first time since his wife's passing and facing the daunting task of raising triplets on his own, he was...optimistic. That's all he would allow himself to acknowledge for now. He and Kelsey had come together because of a shared need, a desperate situation. That could lead to heightened emotions. Once he was fully moved into his own place and things were back to normal, he would see if this fire between them persisted or if it fizzled out.

Punching in the code, Trevor swooped her into his arms and bounded to the rear of the house into the master suite. He dropped her gently in the center of the bed and stepped back. She lifted up on her arms and looked at him. He looked at her, freeze-framing this moment in his mind.

Kelsey looked glorious against those silky white sheets.

Emitting a growl, Trevor fell to his knees. "I'm going to finish what I started today." He removed her shoes and made love to her, tasting and treasuring every delicious inch of her body.

And she screamed. Begging for release.

But he was unyielding. His onslaught continued until she fell apart, overcome with ecstasy.

"That was remarkable," she huffed out, her body slick with sweat.

Trevor settled in next to her on the bed, cradling her in the crook of his arms. He closed his eyes contentedly. "Another satisfied customer," he whispered.

"Your *only* customer," she shot back.

Eyes heavy, he could only smile. Trevor didn't know

how much time passed but he shot up out of his sleep, wide awake, sensations rocking his body.

Kelsey. Sweet Kelsey. Giving all she had. Good grief. She was *relentless*. That was his last coherent thought for quite some time.

Early the next morning, Trevor and Kelsey entered the main house both wearing shades, both ignoring Amy's knowing grin. He had taken a shower, but Kelsey hadn't had a change of clothes, so she was doing the walk of shame.

The triplets greeted them as if they had been gone for weeks instead of mere hours. When those little hands wrapped around his legs, Trevor knew this was the second best moment in the world. The first tied between when he learned he was going to be the father to three children and having Kelsey in his arms.

He took pictures and sent them to his father, this time including Kelsey. Meanwhile, she dashed upstairs to shower and dress for the day. Man, he wished he could join her. But she needed to recoup and there were hungry mouths to feed.

Who is that? Pop was quick to ask.

How did he characterize his emotions for Kelsey? They were grand and exhilarating and complicated. She's someone I'm beginning to care about.

Music to my ears. I needed some good news.

What was he talking about? What's going on Pop? His father merely responded with, Talk soon.
Pop...?

But his father was apparently done talking for the day, and there were three hungry toddlers screaming for some of that cinnamon brown sugar oatmeal that Amy had prepared. It wasn't until late in the afternoon when he was checking on the cattle that he remembered his assistant had sent him a text asking Trevor to call him.

He brought up Graham's contact information and hit the call button. What he heard left him dazed and confused. He had to see Amy immediately. She had some explaining to do.

"Hey, Dad." Kelsey had been too exhausted from her night out with Trevor to head to the ranch today. She needed recovery time after their ardent lovemaking and so had decided to stay home and assist Amy with the children.

Not that she was much help. The sitter had taken the children outside to play in the yard while she lounged on the patio chair. She did, however, spot some beautiful birds that she made a note to mention to Trevor. After her shower, she had dressed in jeans and a floral blouse and had slapped a wide-brimmed hat on her head.

"Hey. I've got to come to your ranch to get a look at that horse soon."

"Yes. Wait until you see her. She's glorious."

Dad took a seat next to her, and she shared pictures of the mare, falling in love with the majestic white beauty all over again.

"Did I tell you that I saw Aaron Walsh the other day?" she asked, making conversation. Also, she didn't want her father bringing up what she and Trevor had almost done in the kitchen. "He was there at the estate when I went to pick up the horse."

"I ran into Aaron as well," her dad said, rubbing his head. "He was asking me if I'd heard anything about the investigation."

"Really?" Kelsey swung her legs to the side and sat up. "That's odd. I know he had already gone to talk to the police, and he said he asked them about the investigation, but they couldn't talk about it. So if the cops aren't saying much, why would he expect you to know about anything?"

Her father shrugged. "He seems on edge. Different. I've known him for a long time, and he isn't himself. He's tense. Nervous."

"Now that you mention it... I agree. He was in such a rush that he sold me the horse without even reviewing my proposal." She placed a hand on her chin. "He's definitely acting different."

"I'm going to do some digging." He pointed at her. "Don't stay out here too long. The sun is vicious today."

"I won't."

Her dad left after that, looking pensive, but Amy called out to her to watch the children while she gave Sasha a diaper change, so Kelsey didn't give that any more thought. Her father would handle things.

Midday, after a lunch of grilled hot dogs, hamburgers and corn, Kelsey must have dozed off, because she felt herself being shook awake. Her skin burned and she was reminded that she hadn't put on any sunscreen. Even though the weather was much cooler, the sun rays were dangerous for her pale skin. She peered into Trevor's worried brown eyes.

"Kelsey, wake up. Your skin looks like it's on fire."

"Where are the children?" she croaked.

"They went down for a nap."

"I'll be fine," she said, clenching her jaw. "This comes with being a redhead. I have ointment in my bathroom to help."

Trevor lifted her in his arms and took her upstairs. Then he applied the balm with such tenderness that she had to hold back tears. He was so thoughtful and kind to her.

"There, now, sweetheart. You should feel better in no time." Trevor drew her into a hug, gingerly kissing her neck and cheek.

"Thank you for helping me." Kelsey wasn't in too much pain, but she would stay inside for the next day or so until her skin cleared up. She leaned backward. "So, what brought you home?"

"I got an interesting call today from my administrative assistant." Trevor rested her on the pillows and paced the room, like a caged animal. That's when it registered that he was upset about something.

"What's going on?" Her heart began to thump in her chest.

"Apparently Amy hasn't cashed any of the checks I've paid her. Not a single one."

Kelsey frowned. "*What?* That makes no sense."

"I thought so too so I came home to talk to her about it. I thought that maybe she was saving them all up for a rainy day, but then..." He bunched his fists. "Ugh, I can't stand that man. I wish he would stay out of my life."

Jumping out of bed, Kelsey went over to grab Trevor's arm. "Trevor, you're not making any sense. What are you talking about?"

"Amy said she wasn't going to double-dip. That Hammond hired her, and he's been paying her salary. She went into her purse and returned the checks."

Kelsey's mouth dropped. "Why didn't she tell you about Hammond before?"

"I didn't ask... I was too livid to think straight once she mentioned Hammond's name."

She scurried out of her room, with Trevor trailing behind her. Kelsey needed to hear what Amy had to say about that. She rushed into the nursery, but the children were asleep. Then she darted down the stairs and into the kitchen, but it was empty.

"Where is she?" she spun around to ask Trevor.

"She's gone." He sat on the bar stool. "I let her go."

"You let her go?" Kelsey asked then raised her voice to demand, "Why in the world would you do that?"

"Because I need someone I can trust to watch my children."

"Amy is the best ever. You said so yourself. We left her overnight with the children just the night before at your urging. And you just *let her go*?" Fury boiled over. "This isn't about her. This is about your anger at your grandfather. I can't believe you."

Trevor folded his arms across his chest. "I told you that I wanted nothing to do with that man."

"*That man* helped you out but you're too stubborn

headed to see that. Now who's going to watch your children?"

He shrugged. "I will."

"Fine job you did with that on your own." She scoffed, placing a hand on her hips. "Did you forget that that's how we met? You were on your own and the children were screaming their heads off. So now you're back to square one."

"I'm not back to square one. I have you."

Kelsey drew in deep breaths, trying to cool her temper. "Thanks for your trust in me, but did you think about the triplets when you sent her away?"

He frowned. "What do you mean?"

"Trevor, they are attached to her. They love her. Don't you think they will miss her?"

"They won't remember her."

Those words cut her deep. She swallowed hard. "So, is that what you're counting on when you leave here at the end of the month? That they will forget me too?"

He came over to hold on to her shoulders. "How can you say that? You mean a lot to them. To me."

"If I do, then why didn't you ask my advice before you fired Amy?" Tears threatened. "Amy is in business for herself. She might not have a job lined up. We don't know much about her, but she could have a family to support. And you just terminated her without a second thought."

Trevor picked up the checks and waved them at her. "Evidence that she's not that desperate. I'm sure my grandfather," he uttered that word through clenched teeth, "took very good care of her. For all I know, she was sent here to spy on me and report back to Hammond all that I'm doing."

"Hammond. Hammond. Hammond. Your hatred for that man has skewed your judgment and your good sense. Why don't you meet with him and hear him out? Life is too short to not forgive family."

"I told you already that man is *not* my family."

Kelsey held up a hand. "We're both passionate people. So, let's take a moment to recalibrate." She took several deep breaths, exhaled and then began again in a much calmer tone. "A great nanny is worth more than gold. You can't pay a person enough for the peace of mind in knowing that your children are in good hands."

"Exactly stated." He lifted his chin and looked down at her through the slits of his eyes. "Those are *my* children. Not yours."

Kelsey gasped, placing a hand on her chest. "I know that, but I love them."

"I know you do but you're young and naive. You're playing house and at any minute you get to decide that you're done playing. I don't have that option. I have three children to care for and I'm all they have. I'm the only person they can truly depend upon."

Sucker punched, Kelsey bent over and clutched her stomach. Her chin wobbling, she looked at him through her tears. "What a hurtful thing to say."

Trevor paced the room. "I've lost my way. I've lost myself in you. I got caught up in this attraction and now I'm too distracted by my feelings for you to think straight."

Her chest concaved. "Wait, are you blaming me for this now?"

"No, I'm blaming myself for allowing this—" he flung his hands in the air "—whatever this thing is between us—to go this far and this long." He exhaled roughly. "I don't think we should see each other anymore."

Though she felt raw and ravaged on the inside, Kelsey stood on her pride. When her mother told her father that she didn't want to be with him, leaving him with Kelsey as a newborn, her father didn't beg her to stay.

Kelsey wouldn't do that either with Trevor. Though her heart was breaking, she refused to let him see it. "If that's what you want to do, I won't stop you."

He studied her for a beat, and for a second, Kelsey thought he would cave, that he would say he made a mistake. But men like Trevor didn't admit they were wrong that easy. He crossed his arms and jutted his jaw. "I'll start packing."

"You expect me to watch the kids while you pack?" Trevor's mouth hung open, as if he had no clue what to say. But of course, Kelsey wouldn't spite the children to harm him. "Don't answer that. I'll watch them." The tears fell then. "It will give me a chance to say goodbye."

"Thanks."

"You can keep your thanks." She curled her lips. "I'm not doing this for you. I'm doing this for *them*."

Hours later, when the house was empty of all his possessions and she heard the happy gurgles of the babies as Trevor toted them out in his arms, blissfully unaware that this was the last time Kelsey would see them, that's when she folded. That's when she curled into herself.

That's when she admitted that she had fallen in love with the most stubborn man in the whole world and she didn't see getting over him anytime soon.

Chapter Twelve

It was close to seventy-two hours since he had moved out of Kelsey's home, since he had been in her arms, and Trevor had had never felt so much regret in his life.

Their parting was very much his doing, but he didn't know it would make him all discombobulated. As a result, he couldn't enjoy his new home. A home he had taken painstaking care to make into his dream abode.

Yet it was the last place he wanted to be, which was why he had canceled his solo Thanksgiving plans. The triplets wouldn't know anyway. He would make himself some noodles or maybe he would pack up the kids, hire a private charter and head to Jamaica or Aruba. Thanksgiving was an American holiday. But walking down the street with the triplets was a lot, so imagine flying international? In short, he needed a new nanny.

Pronto.

Geez, he was being dramatic. He did have family after all. Before he could second-guess himself, Trevor texted Jonathan.

Hey bro. What you up to?

Five minutes later, Jonathan answered. About to have some Porter steaks with the wifey. After a few seconds, another text came through. You good, fam?

Yes. Before he hit Send, Trevor deleted it. Jonathan was his cousin. He could tell him the truth. No. I feel like crap.

His phone rang almost immediately. Trevor sat up and rubbed his eyes. "Hello?"

"What's going on?"

Trevor dared himself to be vulnerable, to be honest. "I'm just feeling alone right now. I met this wonderful woman, and I've screwed things up with her."

"Tell me about her."

He scooted off the bed and clutched the phone to his ear. "But I thought you were about to cook. I don't want to keep you from dinner…"

"Bro, that can wait. We'll order takeout or something. You sound like you need me, and I'm here for you, so get to talking."

Family. His chest puffed. This was what Kelsey was talking about. "Her name is Kelsey, and she's the best thing that has happened to me, and I've ruined it. I've ruined *everything*." Trevor went on to describe how he and Kelsey met and how great she was with him and his children. The more he spoke, the more Trevor realized that his feelings went way past attraction and friendship. He was in love with this woman. And he had mucked everything up.

"She's sounds marvelous. So, what happened, cuz?" The concern in Jonathan's tone touched him.

"We broke up because of Hammond. I allowed my anger at him to destroy what I had with Kelsey."

"I don't get it. What does Grampa have to do with Kelsey?"

Trevor put his phone on speaker then told his cousin about Amy, about Hammond secretly hiring her, and how he fired his sitter when he found out the truth. Finally ending with Kelsey coming at him for letting the nanny go. "I wanted her to be on my side. I wanted Kelsey to understand, to agree with why I couldn't keep Amy on, but she let me have it. She told me I was wrong, and I retaliated by breaking things off. And now I'm miserable. I'm walking around with a hole in my chest."

"Cuz, I feel for you. I really do. But I've got to level with you. You've let anger and unforgiveness chip away at you, at the good man that you are. You've let it rule your mindset and your actions. And as a result, you're allowing my grandfather to have all the power."

"*What?* How am I—"

"Just hear me out, would ya?" Jonathan said.

Trevor huffed out a breath but allowed his cousin to continue.

"Whether you realize it or not, Grampa is dictating where you go and who you hire. You're not in control. That's why you've got to mend fences with him. Like it or not, without him, you wouldn't be here." Jonathan sighed. "How do you think I felt when I learned he had lied to my father and to us? How do you think my grandmother felt knowing the love of her life had had an affair and had hidden three children from her?"

Trevor hadn't thought about that. "I—"

"You think you were the only one hurt by his actions?" Jonathan asked, cutting him off. "I didn't know I had a wonderful cousin who is now a brother to me out there in the world. You don't think I was mad about that? I was furious. I was a ball of hurt. But my grandmother stood by Grampa. She's our family glue. She loves him, flaws and all, and they are stronger than before. They are still together. While you, you are probably hugging your pillow at night when you could have had your woman snuggled up next to you."

Dang. His cousin wasn't mincing his words, but Trevor was man enough to accept the truth. A truth he should have accepted when Kelsey tried to show him.

"What if Kelsey's done with me? What if she doesn't want to see my face?"

"Open your eyes, cuz. The woman you described sounds like she cares about you."

"You have a lot of valid points and you've given me a lot to chew on. Thank you."

"Fix it, fam. Or you're going to grow old with a pile of cash but unfulfilled. Now, get your butt over here for Thanksgiving. You need to be with family."

"I will." His cousin hopped off after that. Jonathan's blunt words were like burning coal on a wound, but Trevor welcomed them, because they were coming from a place of love. Just like Kelsey had done. All the signs were there for how she felt about him. And how he felt about her. But just as he hadn't succeeded in his marriage with Claudia, he had royally messed this up, and Trevor wasn't about to ask for a second chance he did not deserve.

***

Trevor had left his mark everywhere. No matter where she went, Kelsey saw him. In the kitchen, in her bedroom, in the former nursery… He had left an indelible timestamp that punctured her heart.

She couldn't sleep.

Instead, she had roamed the house for hours on end before wandering into her father's wing. Finally, in one of his guest rooms, she had gotten a couple hours of shut-eye. But Kelsey made sure to get up before her dad did and headed out to the ranch, so he didn't know she was now camped out on his side of the house since the breakup. He had asked about Trevor and the children, but she had only said the bare minimum. That his house was ready, and he had left. She didn't have the strength to say any more than that.

Yes, she was avoiding him. Dad would ask too many questions that would get her all in her feelings, and right now, she was in survival mode. She packed her day until she was too exhausted to think, even if she couldn't sleep.

She kept herself busy at the ranch as there was always something to do. And if anybody needed anything, she was the first to volunteer. Today she was going to pay a visit to Priscilla at Liam's Lone Star Ranch, named after Jax's son, where her cousin now resided with her fiancé.

Priscilla wanted to head down to the houseboat that she had inherited from Linc Banning after he was murdered. It was really weird that Linc had left it to Priscilla, considering that they had only been on one date before he had then ended things. So when Priscilla learned that the houseboat was now hers, she had obviously been flabbergasted. The only thing that topped that shock was its deplorable condition.

Kelsey hadn't seen it as yet, but Priscilla had already told her to prepare herself.

Her cousin had decided the best thing to do was renovate it and then sell the houseboat. She was having it professionally cleaned but wanted to give it a final look through. A couple months prior, Priscilla had found a hidden compartment under the bed which had twenty-seven files from the Texas Royale Private Adoption Agency. Priscilla handed the documents over to the police, hoping they might reveal a motive for Linc's murder. So, when Kelsey was asked to accompany her, she had jumped at the chance to play amateur sleuth.

However, Kelsey had a couple hours until their agreed upon meet-up time. Since she had already finished her chores at the ranch and visited with Carmelina, Kelsey decided to stop by the botanical gardens to do some birdwatching. She spotted house sparrows, house finches and blue jays. Kelsey took tons of photos. She was tempted to send them to Trevor, but she deleted his number instead.

That delete was much easier than removing him from her heart. He was really wedged in there. Right next to the triplets. Sigh. If she were going to get over Trevor, Kelsey had to stop thinking about him.

Finally, it was time to meet Priscilla. Her cousin was waiting for her when she pulled up. Jax was with her, his arm slunk about Priscilla's waist, all casual, like it belonged there. That small gesture was almost her undoing, but Kelsey put on the fake cheer and threw them air kisses.

Jax was there to see pictures of the horse. Kelsey got out of the truck to share photos. "I'm jealous. Kudos to you for landing that."

"Come pay me a visit at Fortune 8. I'd love to bend your ear as I'm setting up a riding trail for her."

"For sure," he said.

"Let me know when you want to come, and I'll pencil you in." She needed to keep a full calendar until she had worked Trevor Porter out of her system.

Jax then proceeded to kiss Priscilla like he was a sailor about to deploy overseas. It was intense. Kelsey busied herself by looking at the pictures of the birds on her phone.

Yup. Birds. A poor substitute, but it was all she had now.

"Don't think I don't know what you're doing," Priscilla chided once her fiancé had left, and she was buckled into the passenger seat of Kelsey's truck.

Kelsey put the truck in gear. Since it was a beautiful day, she kept the windows down during their ride downtown. She took the scenic route, using the back roads.

"What do you mean?" she asked, feigning nonchalance as she turned onto the main road.

"Come on, cuz. You're in classic avoidance mode. Packing your day instead of facing that you're hurting over Trevor. What happened with him anyway?" she asked, when Kelsey was stopped at a light.

"This has nothing to do with Trevor." Kelsey had told Priscilla that they had broken up, but she hadn't shared anything more than that. And this wasn't the right moment to do so either.

Her cousin gave her a piercing look before she relented. "Okay, I'll follow your cue." A text pinged her phone. "The cleaning crew is on their way, so you can go a little faster. But catch me up. Has there been any new developments with the secret door you all found at the boathouse?"

"No. Dad's been searching but we haven't found the key to the secret room as of yet."

"That's disappointing. But it's exciting to know that we might finally discover what the hidden family surprise is. All we have to do is find that key."

"Can you believe we have been searching on and off for twenty years?" Kelsey asked in a wistful tone.

"If it weren't for Uncle Sander, I would have given up a long time ago."

"Yeah, my dad can be pretty persistent. But I believe you and your sisters and brother are his motivators. He's driven by the fact that whatever the surprise is, it will be an homage to your parents' legacy."

When they got to the houseboat, since the cleaning crew hadn't arrived yet, Priscilla suggested that they get a final look around. They padded down the short dock and helped each other into the dingy, small floating structure. Dang, this place was in a seriously bad state.

"I don't know if I could live my life with water constantly swaying under me like this," Kelsey said. What she really wanted to say was, *how could someone have lived like this?*

"I don't know. Some find it soothing." Priscilla unlocked the door.

Kelsey wrinkled her nose at the chipped paint and the

loose boards. "Do you know where you want to look? There isn't much to look at."

"No. I doubt we'll find anything, but I would hate it if we missed another clue because I didn't take the time." They walked past the bathroom and she almost gagged. It smelled dusty and moldy. She kept her arms firmly at her sides because she didn't want to touch anything unless she absolutely had to. There was a streak of mildew on the wall, which suggested mold. Sure enough, the porthole had a water stain. Possibly a leak. Her mind grappled to correlate the Linc she had seen in designer wear coming home to such a sorry state.

If only she had known! He could have lived with them in the main house. She wished he had said something. Asked for help. They had more than enough to have been of assistance to him.

"This breaks my heart, cousin," she admitted softly.

"I know. I'm gutted to know Linc was living in this squalor. Imagine what it must have done to his psyche."

"But instead of reaching out for assistance, he must have resented us. Our wealth. Our position." She shuddered.

"Yeah. You never know what's going on with a person on the inside." Priscilla held up her phone and began taking pictures. They walked past the kitchen, which had an odd smell, like rotten food, and traipsed toward Linc's bedroom. As they crossed the threshold, Priscilla tripped over one of the loose boards and her phone skidded into a small space between the headboard and the wall. They walked closer and saw that the phone was just beyond their reach. It was wedged in there real good.

She gestured for Kelsey to get down there. "Do you

mind? I'm not exactly dressed for getting down on my hands and knees."

She'd rolled her eyes earlier when she'd noticed that her cousin was wearing a pristine white jumpsuit—not at all appropriate for the occasion. Whereas Kelsey had donned a more practical ensemble of a light sweater, jeans and walking shoes.

"No can do, cuz. I think I saw a mouse earlier and there might be spiders. And I don't *do* spiders. They can hide out in my hair for days." She shuddered. "Spiders give me the heebie-jeebies."

"Really?"

"Just lay on the blanket and give it a good tug. You won't get dirty." Kelsey squatted and used her phone to light the dim area.

"You expect me to use this grimy blanket?" With a huff, Priscilla kicked off her shoes then stretched out on the mat and reached into the same space. "I've almost got it," she said, drawing a deep breath and giving the phone a pull. "Yes!" Suddenly she leaned in. Kelsey hovered close. "Wait. Hold the light up. Shine it a little to the right. What's that in the wood?"

"What? What do you see?" Kelsey asked, her body poised for flight.

Priscilla scooched a little closer. "There is a weird groove in the headboard." She sat up and gave it a tug. "The headboard is really thick like Linc might have had it specially made. This could be a secret drawer or storage of some kind." She ran a finger over the groove. "It's glued shut. Quick, go get me a screwdriver or something that I can pry this open with."

"Okay, I'll be right back." Kelsey dashed off to the kitchen, grateful to be able to help her cousin. She could see that the stove had the time listed. Grateful there was electricity, Kelsey flipped the switch, then opened the widest kitchen drawer, careful not to snag her sweater against the chipped wood. She dug around in the kitchen drawer, everything cling-clanging in her haste. The drawer had been stuffed with just about everything—menus, matches and, of all things, a tiny axe. What that was doing there, she had no idea, but this was just what was needed.

She ran back to where Priscilla waited. While she was gone, her cousin had opened the lift and shoved the mattress aside. The rest of the bed linens were all bunched together in a heap and the pillows had been tossed to the floor.

She pointed to the thick bulge in the headboard. "See?"

Goose bumps rose on Kelsey's arms. "Wow."

"I know, right." Priscilla grabbed the axe and began to pry the drawer open. Kelsey went to hold the other woman's waist as they tugged. They pulled hard enough to land on their butts. With a snap, the drawer crashed onto the floor beside her, snagging a small thread of Kelsey's pants.

There was a file inside. Kelsey helped Priscilla to stand. She dusted off her pants...which didn't have a spot or wrinkle. *How?* That was the real mystery. The cousins huddled together, eyes zoned in on the manila file. Priscilla bent over and picked it up. On the front was a name written in caps: FINN MORRISON.

"Oh, my goodness, the missing file." Kelsey did a little jump. "That could be his adoption papers!"

"I'm stunned that it's been in here this whole time. If I hadn't dropped my phone..." Priscilla turned the file and saw a name they didn't recognize on the tab. Then when she opened it, she confirmed it was indeed Finn's adoption papers. Her brows furrowed. "That name on the tab must be his birth name." Priscilla closed it and tucked it under her arm. "I'll take this over to Finn as soon as we leave here."

"I wonder what made Linc renege on selling Finn his file?"

Priscilla shrugged. "Maybe he felt some kind of affinity with Finn because they were both outsiders here in town?" She shrugged. "But who knows? Linc wasn't who I thought he was."

"Do you think they resented our wealth?" Kelsey asked. "Finn and Linc?"

"I don't think so. I think they shared a connection in that Delia worked and lived with us and Finn had a summer romance with Zara when they teenagers."

"To be honest, I don't know what Linc was thinking. That man was an enigma..."

Priscilla held up the manila file. "Well, now we're one step closer to solving his murder as well as finding the hidden surprise. That's some good Thanksgiving news. It's just a matter of time before all is revealed."

"I agree. Sooner or later, the truth will make itself known." Kelsey's mind wandered back to the time when Zara dated Finn. Though love hadn't been in the cards for her, Kelsey really wanted to see it work out for someone else. As soon as they were back in her truck, she asked, "Do you think Zara will ever have a second chance with Finn?"

Priscilla chuckled. "That's such a random question. What made you think of that?"

"My thoughts went on a journey…" She shrugged. "And I always wondered what went down with them, but I was too young to ask about it back then. I was like twelve years old when they dated so nobody was telling me anything."

"If I remember right, Finn worked as an attendant at a country club when he was a teenager. That's where he met Zara. They had a great summer romance but then they broke up. Zara does not like to talk about Finn at all. You mention him and she shuts down. In fact, it seems as if they both go out of their way to avoid each other."

"I don't know Finn's reasoning, but I think for Zara, it's because she has *hard feelings* for him."

"What's that's supposed to mean? Feeling are feelings. Period."

"Well, it would be great if the unofficial matchmaker of the family finally found her match."

Chapter Thirteen

At Kelsey's insistence, she and Priscilla headed over to the swanky Emerald Ridge Hotel where Finn had been staying since returning to town.

During the ride over in her truck, Kelsey decided to confide in Priscilla. Trevor filled her mind whether she was busy or not, so she might as well talk about it with family. She described in detail how he had handled the situation with Amy and their ensuing argument over his firing the nanny because of his rift with his grandfather.

"Nothing I said got through to him, but I wasn't backing down. I even told him his children would miss Amy, and he wasn't thinking of them." She gripped the steering wheel. "That's when he went in papa bear mode and told me that I wasn't their mother. I was playing house, and I was a distraction to him. So, he broke things off."

"Oh boy. This is tough." Priscilla adjusted her pants. "Now that a few days have passed, is there anything you would have done differently?"

"No, I don't think so. I told him the truth."

"Truth should be told but it has to be packaged well. It has to be served with a certain level of finesse. You put him on the defensive, and he went into preservation mode."

Since they were on a back road, and no one was behind them, Kelsey slammed on the brake. She looked over at her cousin with disbelief. "Are you seriously defending him?" Her left eye ticked. "The man basically told me I'm a child and too naive to tell him anything."

Priscilla grabbed the handle with one hand and steadied herself. She gripped the manila folder on her leg with the other. "I'm trying to get you to see things from his viewpoint. You're very passionate when you love someone and when you feel you're telling them something that will benefit them."

"Who said anything about *love*?" Kelsey eased her foot off the brake. "Sorry I stopped short like that."

"It's all good. And are you saying you don't love him?"

"Will you stop psychoanalyzing me?" she gritted out. "Of course, I love him, but the man is too stubborn for words."

"Maybe Trevor got thrown for a loop. He sounds like he has good values. I'm sure he'll come around. Take my word, Kelsey, he's going to show up on your doorstep with those puppy dog eyes. And when he does, you'd better let him in."

"Oh, I wouldn't play coy about that. I want him back in my life and I miss those children something fierce."

"Then give him a call. Although, I would say to make him grovel a little though."

"Number one—I deleted his number. And number two? He was the one who broke this off. Which means *he* has to be the one to patch things up. I'm not changing my position on that."

"I hear you."

Kelsey turned into the hotel and handed her car keys over to the valet. "We'll only be a few minutes."

"Okay, I'll park on the side."

They sauntered inside, admiring the modern architecture and the grand surroundings. Priscilla approached the front desk, the manila folder tucked under her arm. Kelsey hung back to admire the waterfall in the center of the reception area.

"I'm here to see Finn Morrison," she said, with an air of authority.

"I'm sorry, Ms. Fortune, but he isn't here. He stepped out about an hour ago."

"Do you have any idea when he will return?" Priscilla asked.

"No, ma'am. But if you want to leave that folder here at the front desk, I can make sure he gets it."

Kelsey stifled a grin, imagining her cousin's reaction to being called a ma'am at twenty-eight years old.

"Thanks for your assistance, but I'll call him. I'd rather hand it over to him personally."

"Okay. Have a great day, ma'am."

"Ready to go, *ma'am*?" Kelsey teased.

Priscilla gave her the side-eye. "Watch it, little lady." Arm in arm, the women returned to pick up her truck. "Do you feel like grabbing lunch?" Priscilla asked.

"I'd love to, but I'm not exactly dressed for dining in." She wondered what the triplets would have for their lunch today—sweet potatoes? Chicken and rice? It seemed unlikely that Trevor would have found a replacement for Amy that fast, so he was most likely back to tackling feeding time on his own. Then she reminded herself that Trevor's children were no longer her concern.

Priscilla asked a question that bore into her thoughts. "Do you think that when I meet up with Finn to hand over the file, I should ask him how he thinks his parents afforded the adoption fees?"

"No. That's way too personal. And it comes off a little Karen-like. Almost entitled."

Priscilla's mouth dropped. "Does it? You know that's not my intention."

"I know, but he doesn't know that. People are funny when you talk about money. Or rather, the disparities between the haves and have-nots." Kelsey patted Priscilla's arm. "Just deliver the file. I have a feeling the truth will come out eventually."

"Yep. It always does. It's just a matter of time."

"Kelsey!" a voice called out from behind her.

She had just dropped Priscilla off and had stopped by the farmers market for more fruit and veggies when she heard that unmistakable tenor.

Kelsey turned to see her father waving a hand, meandering through the bustling crowd to get to where she stood at the entrance of the market. In the final days before Thanksgiving, she knew there would be plenty of last-minute shoppers, but she hadn't expected so many people would be here. When he was a few feet away, he jogged over in his running shorts and T-shirt. One of the few times her father was without his trademark Stetson. Dad planted a kiss on the cheek. "I thought that was you."

"Hey, Dad." She mumbled, curling her basket around her arm. "How's pickleball going?" Kelsey picked up carrots, and she couldn't forget she needed lots of Granny Smith apples.

"Meh." He shrugged. "I'm not sure how much longer I'll keep going though. We'll see. I was on my way there and decided to stop here for some of those roasted pecans." He patted his stomach.

"Well, the whole point of a hobby is that you can start and stop as you please." She went in search of some organic honey, hoping she didn't come off as frosty.

Her father took the basket to carry it for her and draped his free arm about her shoulder. "What's going on with you lately? You haven't been yourself since Trevor left, and we're like two ships in the night. By the time I get up most mornings, you're already gone. If I didn't know better, I would think you were avoiding me."

Guilt made her tense up. She might as well fess up. "Trevor decided it was best we parted ways, and I've been trying to handle it in my own way."

"Oh, honey. I'm sorry to hear that."

"Are you? I imagine you might be secretly relieved that I'm not running after three babies."

Her father placed a hand on her arm. "All I want for you is to be happy. That's all." He leaned in to give her a hug. "I'm here if you need me."

Kelsey allowed herself to be comforted for a few seconds but then she pulled away. If she stayed in her father's arms, then she would fall apart. So, she switched topics. "I'm glad that I ran into you actually. I was just with Priscilla, and we were just at her houseboat to give it a last search before she has it professionally cleaned."

"Did you find anything?" he asked.

"Yes, there was a secret drawer underneath Linc Banning's bed."

His brows shot up. "Seriously? What did you find?"

"Finn Morrison's adoption papers."

"Whoa." Dad dropped his voice to a whisper. "Do you think Linc was trying to sell those to Finn?"

"That's what we think. But right now, we have more questions than answers."

Trevor hadn't slept for a solid hour the night before. Every hour on the hour one of the triplets had awakened. Nothing he said or did soothed them. He sang lullabies until he was hoarse, but as soon as he put one down another got started.

It's like they had staged a coup and until he brought Amy and Kelsey back, they were going to challenge his sanity. Right now, he was moving off fumes.

Logically, Trevor knew that the triplets were just being fussy babies, but he been pushed to the end of the rope and there was nothing but a deep, rocky, backbreaking crevice beneath him.

Now he had three sleepy, hungry babies who each wanted to be rocked and held. Desperate, Trevor had called Jonathan, but his cousin had laughed—*actually laughed*—and said, "You know what to do," before pressing the end button.

He didn't have the guts to call Kelsey. He didn't deserve her.

But Amy had been a faithful employee. He could probably fix that, so he called and invited her to come over. Even if he had to grovel and beg, Trevor was going to get her back. He paced by the front door, peeking out the windows, while awaiting her arrival. Suddenly, a little bum landed on his shoe, capturing his attention.

Soon Trevor heard a car door slam and then Amy was at his door. Trevor swung it open before she could ring the doorbell. By this time, he had William in one arm, Sasha by his hip and James sitting on one foot.

As soon as they saw her, two sets of hands reached for her. And William bopped Trevor on the head. Amy hid a giggle behind her hand. "I would ask how you are, but I can see that you could use a hand."

"Tell me about it," he muttered, moving out of the way to let her in.

She reached down to pick up Sasha, who gave Amy a big hug. That alone cemented it for Trevor that he had made the right decision in asking her to come back. His pride was not worth his children's happiness.

Amy rubbed noses with Sasha. "I've missed you, sweet girl." Then she looked at Trevor. "I've missed all of you."

They went into the kitchen and Amy glanced around. "Your new home is beautiful, Trevor."

"Thank you. And there is room here for you if you're still available."

"Oh?" Her eyes held genuine interest.

"Yes, there is a guesthouse with its own private driveway that might suit your needs. If you'll come back." Thinking of the fact that he had planned to offer it to his father, Trevor reasoned he would build Pop a house instead.

"Yes, I'm available, and I've been going stir-crazy at home. Your grandfather refused to stop paying. Said you'd come to your senses, and he didn't want me booked up when you do."

"Hammond Porter is a smart man. I never thought I'd say this, but I'm glad he went behind my back and found you. But I will take over paying for your salary." Trevor knew he would have to thank his grandfather personally as well. His stomach protested at that realization but…baby steps.

"Hammond said you'd say that." She held out a hand. "I accept. And I'll take you up on that offer for the guesthouse."

"Great. Then it's settled."

Sasha pushed herself out of her arms to join James, who had waddled off to pick up something off the floor and stick into his mouth. It looked like a piece of fruit. He hoped.

"Looks like they are hungry," she murmured, rolling up her sleeves. "I'll fix them something to eat."

"That would be great." She stood to move toward the pantry, but he held her arm. "But first, Amy, I want to apologize. I acted in haste, and I appreciate how gracious you are to return."

"I understand." Her eyes held a little sadness. He wanted to know what her story was, but Trevor would respect her privacy. "Family can be complicated." She looked around then tipped her chin at him. "As I said, you have a lovely home. I firmly believe a home is all about the people not a place."

He narrowed his eyes. Was she talking about Kelsey or was he reading too much into her statement? Trevor couldn't be sure. But within an hour, his children had been fed dinner, his house was in order and now they were all asleep. Trevor jogged into his study and returned with her uncashed checks.

"I don't need that. I just need people to care about who care about me."

His heart stirred. "Well, you have that in abundance." He put the checks in her hand. "Consider this a bonus."

Since the triplets were in bed for the night, he decided to take a much-needed nap. He didn't get up until close to midnight and that was only because his cell phone beeped.

Son, I'm sorry to put you out but I need you to come get me.

Heart thumping, Trevor sprang out of bed. He tried to call his father, but it went to voicemail. He sent a text. Pop, where are you? He pulled up the location app, hands shaking. Shoot, his father never accepted the invite. He gripped his hand. What was he going to do? Amy had gone home and wouldn't be moving in until the beginning of next month.

He tried his father again but didn't get an answer. "Hey, Pop. I got your message but I'm having trouble reaching you. Please call me back." He sat for a few minutes waiting, but he couldn't just sit and do nothing. For all he knew, Pop might have lost the cell phone signal.

Trevor told himself not the panic, but his father wouldn't have reached out if it wasn't an emergency of sorts. *Think, Trevor, think.*

The itinerary! He snatched his laptop off the nightstand and logged into his email. His shoulders deflated. His father should still be at sea, but if he left early in the morning, he would catch the ship when it docked at the Cayman Islands. Feeling good that he at least had a semblance of a plan, Trevor searched for the private charter he had used in the past. Usually, Graham would handle these details, but he wasn't going to wake his assistant at this hour.

The charter company had a twenty-four-hour call line. But when he phoned them, as unbelievable as it sounded, they were all booked. Some tycoon was getting married and had rented out all the charter jets to fly his guests to the Maldives.

This can't be happening!

When this was all over, he was going to buy himself a jet. Trevor didn't do a lot of overseas travel, so he generally flew first-class. But this was an emergency, and the airport was a good distance away.

Suddenly, he stilled. Hammond. The old man had a private charter. All he had to do was call. He slammed a fist on his thigh. Hammond was his quickest path to Pop, and he needed to stop procrastinating and get on it.

Despite the hour, he called his grandfather. Hammond picked up immediately.

"Hello, sir, I'm sorry to call this late—"

"I wasn't sleeping. Are the babies alright?" Hammond

asked, cutting him off. The concern in his voice caught Trevor off guard.

"Y-yes. It's my father. He's on a month-long cruise and—"

"The hour is late. Spit it out, son. What do you need?" Hammond demanded.

"A jet."

"Do you have enough space on that land of yours?"

"Yes," Trevor said.

"It'll be there within the hour."

"Wait, do you need my address?"

"I've got it." The line went dead.

That was unbelievably easy. Now he just had one more call to make. The hardest one yet. He picked up his cell phone and paused before resting it on his knee. This one needed a much more personal touch. If he hurried, he would be there and back before the charter arrived.

Chapter Fourteen

Insomnia was a pain. Kelsey roamed the house, pleading with sleep to come. She rued this silent torture with sleep as the elusive prize.

But there are times when her insomnia was a gift, like when her doorbell rang half past midnight, just as she was about to start a rom-com marathon.

Kelsey rushed to answer the door, thinking it might be one of her cousins. Her father was probably sound asleep by now. When she saw who stood there, her eyes went wide. "Trevor?" She wrapped her robe around her tightly as the temperatures had fallen. Beside him, the children were asleep in the wagon. "You brought the children out here at this time of the morning?" She fussed to cover her internal relief. "What's the matter with you? What is it that you have to say that couldn't wait until morning?"

"I, uh, I wasn't thinking. But I need your help."

"Get in here. There's a draft." She ushered him inside along with the children and shut the door. At least he'd had the good sense to put them in sweaters, but they were all in their jammies.

Trevor dropped the baby bag on the floor. She took in the sleeping triplets. It had only been a couple days, but they looked bigger. They wouldn't all fit in the wagon for long. Her heart constricted. "Aww. I've missed them." Kelsey bent over and gave them soft kisses. She looked up at Trevor, standing there looking pitiful, his arms draped at his side. "What are you doing here?"

"I have a lot going on right now. I don't even know where to start."

His puppy dog face made her want to throw her arms around him and tell him that whatever it was, they would work it out together. But the man had callously tossed her out of his life. She wasn't going to make it easy on him.

"How about you start with an apology?" She injected steel into her voice.

He stepped close to her. "I'm sorry. I'm so, so sorry."

Aww. He looked woeful, but she wouldn't cave. She flecked a piece of cotton on her robe. "So, this is where I'm supposed to…what?" Trevor looked at his watch. She shook her head in disbelief. "Oh, am I keeping you from something?"

He let it all out in one whoosh. "Kelsey, I know we have to have this talk and I'm more than willing to eat humble pie and anything else you need me to, but my father is in trouble and I have to go and there is no one, *absolutely no one*, that I trust more than you with my children because, as you say, family is everything. So, I am hoping for their sake—" he held up his hands "—not mine, that you would take care of my most precious possessions for me until I return."

She placed a hand on her chin. "Wow. I'm impressed you did that in one breath."

"I see that I've wasted my time. I'm sorry to intrude."

Trevor reached for the wagon handle. "I'll get out your hair." His long legs ate up the distance to the front door.

"Don't you dare take those children back out there," she said. "I was trying to be cute and pretend to be unaffected that you're here, but I took it too far." She gave him a sheepish look. "Obviously, you wouldn't be here at this time in the morning if it wasn't important, and I shouldn't have minimized that in any way. What's going on with your father?"

"I don't have all the details, but Pop sent me a text asking me to come get him. He hasn't answered my calls or messages since then and I'm truly worried about him. I don't know what to think." He ran a hand over his head. "But I'm heading to the Cayman Islands. According to the trip schedule, that's where he should be. I have to leave in—" he peered at his watch again "—twenty-four minutes."

"Oh no. I'm so sorry I was clowning around when your father could be in trouble. That sounds scary. Go, take care of your business. I'll be praying for good news concerning your dad. We'll talk when you get back."

"Thanks so much. My grandfather is coming to get me. In his private charter."

She raised a brow. "Your grandfather? Hammond Porter?"

"Yes, I called him for help. And I've rehired Amy earlier today. I'll let her know to report here in the morning, but I hope to be back by then."

Whoa. A lot had happened in the past forty-eight hours, but now wasn't the time to press for information. Kelsey placed a hand on her chest. "I'm so proud of you,

Trevor. And I'm honored you've entrusted me with your triplets' care. I'll take care of them like they're my own. Be safe and hurry back."

Now, if this were the movies, before the hero rushed off to do what needed to be done, he would give the heroine a kiss. Right before she closed the door, Trevor hesitated. He looked like he wanted to kiss her, and, oh, she wanted him to, but this wasn't a Hollywood flick. Just because Trevor was asking her for help, Kelsey couldn't presume that meant he wanted them to get back together. She swallowed her disappointment and wished him well.

Trevor gave her a little wave and she closed the door. Heading over to the babies, she couldn't hold back her smile. That's when she truly heard Trevor's words... *There is no one, absolutely no one, that I trust more than you with my children because, as you say, family is everything...* She sucked in a deep breath. At first listen, she thought he had been talking about his father, but he had been talking about her. Trevor saw her as family. *His family.*

Her composure cracked.

She crumbled to the floor as the tears flowed. Tears of hope. Tears of joy. Tears of love.

Trevor had spent the last thirteen years abhorring this man, yet he had never seen Hammond Porter face-to-face.

So, his first impression of seeing his grandfather in person, after getting over the shock that he had shown up with the charter, was that Hammond was not what he had imagined. From what he had read online, Trevor knew that the only black billionaire in Texas was an octogenarian, but he hadn't expected Hammond to seem so sprightly and fit.

After a whispered, "You look so much like your mother," Hammond had grabbed his travel bag and swung it like it weighed less than a pound into the overhead compartment. And Trevor hadn't packed light.

He had brought a change of clothes and toiletries for his father and himself. Since his father hadn't mentioned Manuela, Trevor assumed that his fiancée was alright. The interior of the luxury craft accommodated up to seven people, with beige carpeting and cream-colored leather seats that reclined. Very swanky. Not that he'd expected anything less from Hammond Porter. The dark oak furniture was handcrafted with marquetry and crystal, and there was a minibar and kitchen in the rear, along with two bathrooms. Trevor also noted that there was a staff of three besides the pilot.

Hammond pierced him with a discerning gaze. "We have close to a seven-hour flight. How about we get some shut-eye? I can answer any questions you have once we're rested."

"Okay, sir."

"No need to be so formal, son."

"I don't know you like that, sir."

Hammond's eyes shuttered. "You don't know how much I regret that." He looked outside the window into the darkness of the night. "I regret a *lot* of things."

That comment begged for further explanation, and it wasn't explored until 7:00 a.m. when both Trevor and Hammond awakened. He woke at that time, the unmistakable scent of bacon in the air, more out of habit than anything else. Eyes like his mother's studied him.

"We have about an hour before we land. Breakfast is about ready," his grandfather told him.

Trevor excused himself to wash up. When he returned, one of the attendants came bearing two steaming mugs of coffee, followed by two huge plates of steak, eggs, turkey bacon and bowls of fresh fruit. "Zuri's not here so I'm sneaking in a piece of Porter Cuts," Hammond said, referring to his wife. The older man said grace and they dug in.

"Let me start by thanking you for the ride," Trevor began, cutting into his succulent piece of steak. "And for supporting Porter Cuts."

"You're family, son, and that means everything to me."

"Really?" he scoffed. "Then I guess my mother wasn't family, judging by the way you cut her off." Anger flooded through his tone. He stuffed his mouth with eggs to keep from spewing more.

Hammond leaned forward. "I admit I handled that whole situation wrong. I threatened to cut her off if she married Orson, but she called my bluff. Turns out your mother had a will of steel. They eloped not too long after. But I couldn't bear to see my child suffer in any way, so I approached Orson. Samira saw it as my way of trying to control her." He waved his fork. "And she turned on Orson in the process. She never gave either of us a chance again."

"You could have made things right," Trevor protested. "As long as I live, I will never forget my mother dying alone. You didn't come to her bedside." Resentment resurfaced and his appetite vanished. He pushed his plate to the side. "You didn't come to her funeral."

Hammond shook his head. "Samira refused any assistance from me. I hired a team of doctors, and she turned them away."

"I don't believe you," Trevor snapped.

Hammond slumped, looking every bit of his eighty-odd years. Standing up, he reached in the overhead space for an oblong metal box and handed it to him. "What's this?"

"Open it up."

He lifted the lid. Inside there were stacks and stacks of letters, cards and some papers. The letters and cards hadn't been opened. Most were stamped Return to Sender. Picking up a random card, Trevor saw that they were addressed to his mother. "You wrote her?"

"Yes, and you. It's all in there. Birthday cards, Christmas cards...handwritten letters. The papers are an outline of a health care regimen to aggressively treat her cancer that I had my assistant deliver. But Robin was unsuccessful."

Trevor reviewed the documents. "I don't believe it. Why would my mother refuse this level of treatment if it would have helped her?" Had she hated her father that much?

"I suppose she had her reasons. But I do believe she thought she was protecting you. Money can lull you into thinking that you can do whatever you want. That's what it did to me. But there are repercussions in everything you do, son. Sometimes you lose out and you never get the chance to gain it back." There was no hiding his deep regret. "I lost my precious girl, and I never got the chance to mend fences with her."

Once again, Kelsey's question came back to him. *So did she tell you to hurt you, or did she hope for something more?* "The last person my mother talked about was you."

"She did?"

"I don't why she did that. But maybe in her own way, Mom wanted me to reach out. I would have been truly alone if I didn't reunite with Pop and if I didn't find Jonathan and Imani." Trevor lifted his shoulders. "I can't speak on her motives, but I do know I don't want to continue blaming you for her death. I don't want to walk around with all this anger festering inside me. And I don't want to pass any of this onto my children." He lowered his eyes. "Cancer is a greedy predator that doesn't discriminate." His voice cracked. "All I know is that I miss my mom. I miss her every single day. And I needed her. I needed her every day after that. And even after all these years, I still need her now."

Trevor's shoulders shook from the weight of his grief. Sorrow engulfed him. A pair of hands encircled him. Grabbing on to his grandfather, Trevor let the floodgates open. Hammond rocked him in his arms, soothing and comforting him, and Trevor soaked it all in. Even as his tears soaked through Hammond's designer shirt. It was some time before he pulled away.

"I'm sorry I fell apart like that." He reached for a tissue and wiped his eyes.

"I'm glad you had a good cry. Tears are cleansing.

They lead to new beginnings." Returning to his seat, Hammond dabbed at his own eyes. "I did come to the funeral, but I didn't have the courage to come inside."

Trevor was shocked. "You were there?"

"Yes. Robin came outside, and I watched the short ceremony from his iPhone." His eyes welled. "My only comfort is that she did *not* die alone. She had you."

Oh, wow. His grandfather was right. He *had* been there. Trevor straightened, his chest lighter. "You're right. She had me, and for Mom, maybe that was enough." He drew in a deep breath though. "It isn't for me though. I need a circle." He broke into a smile. "That's it. That's why Mom told me about you. She knew that one day, I might need you. I might need family, and she wanted me to know that you were there, just in case." Trevor grew emotional. "Even from her deathbed, Mom was looking out for me."

The captain announced that they were landing.

"I can see that. A mother's love is the sweetest, purest gift," Hammond said once the captain was finished talking. "And Samira's right. I'm here for you, son. As long as I'm breathing, I always will be."

Hammond used his connections to put out feelers on Pop's location, so by the time they landed, his grandfather knew exactly where Pop would be.

Trevor was too relieved to question those connections, especially since his grandfather's explanation was, "I know a man or two."

As it turned out, Pop never left Barbuda. He had contracted a severe case of the flu, and after a couple days of confusion, high fevers and diarrhea, he had been admitted to the hospital and placed in intensive care. That explained why Trevor hadn't heard from him for a few days. And Pop himself called Trevor, trying to protect him by withholding this information.

When they walked in, Manuela, who had been asleep in the corner of the room, had jumped up with obvious relief. She was a petite woman, her dark hair streaked with gray, with light crow's feet around her eyes. She wore a yellow shirt and a pair of white capris as well as some slip-ons. "I had to put my foot down for Orson to reach out for your help. He's been on antibiotics and is getting better, but I think he needs to go home." She assured him that she never left his father's side and that his father was indeed over the worst of it.

"I'm weak. But I'm better, son," Pop croaked out, holding out his arms. His tall frame appeared almost skeletal. Pop had shaved his head and had a small goatee before he left, but his full beard had grown in.

Trevor had been too shaken to move at first. Pop had lost a lot of weight. It was startling and triggering. It was like seeing his mother on her deathbed all over again. Trevor was glad for Hammond's calming presence.

At Hammond's urging, he went over to hug him. "I'm glad you're okay, Pop. I couldn't bear the thought of losing you so soon after getting to know you."

"It's alright, son. God has other plans." Pop patted Trevor's back.

Trevor swallowed a lump in his throat. "Next time, please don't leave me hanging like that. I could have gotten here sooner to help you." He looked over at Manuela. "We're going to exchange numbers so you can reach out to me. Thank you for taking care of him and not leaving his side."

Pop looked between Trevor and his grandfather and whispered, "My heart is glad to see you two have reconciled." The tears rolling down the side of his dad's face was his undoing.

"Hush, Pop. I'll tell you all about that when you have your strength back."

Hammond took charge, and in less than two hours, all four of them were back on the charter jet heading back to Emerald Ridge. Turns out one of the staff onboard the flight was a physician. Hammond had brought him along, just in case.

"Say you'll come to Thanksgiving breakfast at Chatelaine Hills," his grandfather said. He gestured toward Pop and Manuela a few feet behind them. "All of you."

Trevor nodded. "I'll be there. I mean, we'll all be there. As long as Pop is able." Then he straightened and looked Hammond in the eyes. "Thank you for not hesitating when I called, despite my abominable behavior toward you. I'm grateful for all you did to help me and my father today."

His grandfather was visibly moved. "Anything for you, son. I just wish I'd have had the same chance with Samira. I'll take that regret to my grave."

Trevor didn't know how to comfort him about that, but he could offer some measure of peace. "We can't change the past, but we can brighten the future."

"Where did you hear that?"

"From my mom. She said it all the time."

Hammond smiled. "It's something I used to say to her and her siblings."

"Oh wow. I had no idea."

His face softened before he changed the subject. "I'm looking forward to finally meeting my great-grandchildren. Do you have any pictures?"

"Amy didn't send you any?"

"Not a single one. She refused to be a spy, no matter how much I pleaded."

"Wait, are you telling me you have no idea what the triplets look like?" His respect for Amy was now higher than the elevation of this aircraft.

"No. I've searched the internet but you're not a social media man."

"Say no more." Trevor pulled up his phone and moved to sit by Hammond's side. "You don't know what you did asking a proud father if he has photos of his kids. If you want pictures, I've got pictures. I've got enough to last this entire plane ride."

Hammond grinned. "Bring it on."

Chapter Fifteen

The children had just gone down for their afternoon nap when the doorbell rang, and Kelsey found herself once again looking into the beseeching brown eyes of Trevor Porter. He was dressed in a flannel shirt, his cowboy hat and denim jeans. There were lines of tiredness around his eyes, but other than that, he looked calm.

"You're back," she breathed out, thinking of the chicken gravy on her blouse and jeans.

"How are the children?" he asked, flicking a piece of rice off her blouse. She and Amy had fed the children rice and baked chicken for lunch. She must look a sorry sight, but at least she'd fished the chicken pieces out of her hair, though she imagined it would need a good washing. Sasha and James had both been playing with her hair.

"They're fine... Sleeping. We just fed them lunch..." He beckoned her outside. "How about we take a walk? I could stretch my legs after being in the air for close to fourteen hours."

Kelsey called out to Amy to let her know she was leaving the house and then she slipped outside. Trevor reached for her hand. But she clasped her hands together. As they walked, she engaged in small talk—keeping it about the triplets. "The trail to the boathouse is nice this time of year. Lots of fall foliage. The kids had a great time playing in the leaves. There were leaves everywhere by the time they were done."

He laughed. "Thank you for taking care of them."

"You're quite welcome. It was my pleasure. I'd do anything for those kids. How's your father doing?"

"He was very sick. But he's home and on the mend." Trevor paused mid-stride to look at her. "Can we stop tiptoeing around each other as if we're polite strangers? I've got plenty I need to get off my chest."

"Alright, what do you have to say?" She pinched her lips tight.

"I..." He cleared his throat. "Give me a minute. I'm nervous."

That kindled her ire. "Why? You don't seem to have a problem speaking your mind when you have something insulting and hurtful to say," she tossed back at him.

Trevor had the decency to look ashamed. "You're right."

Kelsey avoided eye contact because he looked so woeful that her heart begged her to cave. But shoot, this man had hurt her so. He needed to squirm a little because every time she thought about him carelessly tossing her out of his life, it cut her a little deeper than before.

Along with her realization of the love she had for him came the knowledge that he could use that for his benefit—if she allowed it. And Kelsey wasn't going to be anyone's pawn.

"The last time I saw you, I mentioned how much I

trusted you with my kids. Well, it's the same when it comes to my heart. Kelsey, I—"

Her cell buzzed, interrupting Trevor mid-speech. It was Nancy calling, plus there was a text message asking Kelsey to call her. She held up a finger in Trevor's direction. "I'm sorry, I have to take this."

"Can it hold for another minute?" He wiped his brow.

There was another buzz. "Just let me…" She pressed the phone icon and said hello. What she heard, made her do a jig with glee. "Are you sure?" she asked Nancy.

"Positive."

"Okay, I'll be right there."

She stalked toward her house and rushed upstairs to grab her emergency duffle bag, while Trevor beelined to look in on his children. As soon as she dashed back downstairs, he was on her heels.

"What's going on?" he huffed out. "We weren't finished with our conversation."

"It can hold. My ewe is lambing for real this time and I've got to get over to the ranch. Nancy said she had to call the vet because it looked like the ewe was bleeding a lot." Nancy had advised her to pack an overnight bag with essentials in case she ended up needing to spend the night. Kelsey was sure glad that she had listened.

"You're right. You've got to get out of here. Whatever I have to say can wait until I have your full attention. Mind if I tag along?"

"Aren't you jetlagged?"

"If you don't want me sharing this moment with you, just say so." His tone held a measure of disappointment.

See now. Why did he have to put it like that? Kelsey

placed a hand on his arm. "I was only looking out for you because you have been traveling for hours. But you're more than welcome to come. In fact, you can drive. I'm way too jumpy now to get behind the wheel." She took a moment to let Amy know their plans, then thanked Trevor, who held open the door for her.

A grueling three hours later, the baby lamb made its grand entrance in the world.

As Kelsey and Nancy watched the ewe lick her baby clean, Trevor watched Kelsey. The vet had long since departed for another ranch once the ewe was out of danger. Kelsey's face shone with happiness and contentment, and all he could think was, he so did not deserve this woman. But if she gave him a second chance, he would do his best to keep her smiling.

She turned to face him and his heart skipped a beat.

He held out his hand. After a brief hesitation, she walked over and placed her hand in his.

Nancy crooked her head at them. "Go on home. I've got this." With a brief nod, they departed.

"That was the most beautiful thing I have ever seen," Kelsey breathed out once they were out of the barn.

"I'm seeing better," he said tenderly, touching her hair. He didn't dare follow his urge to kiss her.

She blushed. "You've got to be ready to pass out."

His eyes felt like sand, but there was no place else that he would rather be. "I'm glad I was here to soak in this moment with you. I can see how much you love ranching."

"Can you blame me?" Kelsey threw her arms open

wide and twirled. "I have a slice of heaven here—the vast land, the beautiful sunsets and I get to experience the awesomeness of nature firsthand. I just watched a baby lamb take its first breath, its first step." She inhaled. "It's scary and thrilling at the same time. There's nothing like it."

There was. But she didn't know it yet.

A memory of Claudia bonding with their children flashed before him. The doctors had rested the three small bundles against her chest right after delivery. She had been exhausted but had given him a beautiful smile and said, *My life is now complete.* Trevor had been too choked up to do more than nod.

He imagined her belly swelled with her child and knew he wanted to be the one to give her that precious gift. If she would have him. But he had hurt her and Trevor knew he had work to do to get their relationship back on track.

"What can I do to make things right with you?" he whispered, contrite.

Her eyes filled. "Just don't shut me out. Don't shut me out when things get hard. And don't shut me out of your children's lives." Her voice broke.

Gosh, he had really caused her pain. Trevor wiped away the tears from her eyes. "I won't do it again."

Kelsey stepped closer. "My heart isn't your yo-yo. You don't get to play with it and toss it aside."

Her words pierced his chest. He was an ogre for making her feel this way. Trevor gathered her close and repeated his words. "I won't do it again," then added, "I'm sorry."

"Good," she sniffled before shoving out of his arms. "I need to take Carmelina for a ride. I could use a change of scenery." He swallowed his jealousy. He had no reason to be jealous of a horse.

"Alright. How much time do you need?" He backed away. "I can come back to get you later if you'd like. It's going to be dark soon..." His stomach grumbled, reminding him that he hadn't eaten in hours.

"Silly. Silly. You're coming with me."

"Oh, you want me to come with?"

"Yeah."

"Oh, I'm down with that. Any chance you'll let me ride Carmelina?"

"Nope." Grabbing his hand, they raced toward the shed. "You can ride Kahlua."

In no time, they had the horses saddled and ready to go. Trevor was glad to let Kelsey lead. Just as they neared the trail, Kelsey leaned forward, her butt perched in the air. "C'mon, I'll take you to my secret spot."

"A secret spot? Oh, now I'm intrigued." In a flash, they were off. By the time they arrived at their destination—a shed tucked behind some huge trees—it was close to 4:00 p.m. His stomach was good and ready now to eat. He dismounted, assisted Kelsey off her horse, before securing them, and then took in the view. The expanse of the land, the greenery, the oranges and hues of the skies made his breath catch. "Majestic."

Kelsey bobbed her head. "Exactly how I feel every time I come out here." The horses munched on the grass.

"Did you build this?" he asked, jutting his chin toward the shed.

"Yes. After my third time getting caught out here in the rain, I put this up." She reached into her jeans and took out a key. "Let's go inside."

As soon as she opened the door, the tantalizing scent of food hit his nostrils. There was a picnic basket on the small table in the corner of the room, along with a bed and a small bathroom. "This isn't a shed. It's a tiny home."

She shrugged. "We Fortunes do love our amenities."

"When did you do all this?" he asked, going over to open the basket.

"During the drive over to the ranch." She giggled. "Nancy's son, Nathan, helped me out."

"Oh, so this isn't a secret spot then."

"Yeah, I guess not. But Nathan has been a great help so far. Especially once he learned he was earning a salary."

"That's wonderful. Well, my tummy is thanking you and him right now."

"I figured you'd be hungry."

Trevor's heart warmed at her thoughtfulness. While they ate, his eyes strayed to the bed. He wouldn't mind curling up with Kelsey and catching up on his sleep. But he desperately wanted to take a shower and get under his own covers. Hopefully, Kelsey would be amenable to joining him… But first, he needed to continue the conversation he had started hours prior.

Finishing up his meal, Trevor wiped his hands with the disposable napkins and gulped down the rest of his water. Then he slipped to his knees.

Kelsey almost pounced out of her chair. "Wh-what are you doing?"

"Relax. It's not what you think." He looked into her eyes. "As I was saying earlier, I've entrusted you with my kids and now I'm doing the same with my heart. Kelsey, I'm in love with you, and if you give me a second chance, I'll never make you doubt my feelings for you or your significance in my life again."

She dabbed at her eyes and nodded. "I love you too." Then she gave him a brief hug. "Now get up off your knees and kiss me. The next time you do that..."

He broke into a smile. "Trust me, the next time I do that, it won't be because I'm apologizing. And that's a promise."

Then he drew her in for a kiss, and all he could think was how kissing Kelsey felt like coming home. His only question was, where would be home for her?

Chapter Sixteen

Trevor Porter was about to propose. From the moment he had shown up to her door dressed in a new pair of jeans, shirt, boots along with a fresh haircut, she'd had a feeling. A feeling confirmed when Trevor stood by the doorjamb, holding flowers, looking unsure, and mighty cute.

Good thing was she was also looking cute in her polka-dot sundress this morning. So she was ready to hear what he had to say.

After a beat, Trevor puffed his chest. "I knew when I first met you that you were a swan, the Queen's bird, distinctive, a standout. But what I *didn't* know was that I had met a woman as selfless as the African gray parrot and one as industrious as the wren. Because if I had known all that, I would have danced like the red-capped manakin knowing that I had found my very own paradise tanager. And just as the paradise tanager is the jewel of the rainforest, you, Kelsey Fortune, are the jewel of my heart. Like the robin, you took my little cowbirds in and cared for them as your own, and that means the world to me."

Kelsey wiped her eyes. Her heart was like butter. "That has to be the corniest, sweetest thing anyone has said to me."

"I'm not done yet." He took her hand in his and continued. "I love you, Kelsey, and it would be the honor of my life if you agreed to be my mate for life. Will you be a mother to my children? My bird-watching partner, my lover, best friend and the keeper of my heart?"

She covered her mouth with her hands. "I love you too, Trevor, and I love those precious children. So, yes, yes, I'll marry you." Standing, Trevor kissed her with such passion and hunger that they pulled apart, gasping for air.

"Later?" Trevor asked.

"Actually. Now that we are engaged, I'd like to wait until we're married."

His face looked crestfallen, but he said, "Okay. Whatever you want to do."

They locked lips again, but Kelsey pulled away before things got too heated between them. "Restraint, remember?"

"Got it." Trevor put some space between them and rubbed his head. "I'll have your ring soon. The jewelry store mistakenly ordered the wrong size, but I couldn't wait any longer to propose. It will be worth the wait, I promise."

Kelsey looked at her bare left hand. "You know, I was so caught up, I didn't even register you didn't have one."

"Now, I do have one more question. Where will we live? My place or yours? I know I just built that house, but home is where you are. I'm prepared to nest wherever you want."

"Thank you for that, Trevor. I admit that I'm really torn. I've been dreaming of living on my own ranch for years. But I've had so much input on the house with you that I'm invested in it as much as you are. Especially since it's perfectly suited for the children." She slipped her arms through his. "Can you give me some time to think about it?"

"Sure. Take all the time you need."

"I know I'm doing things backward," Trevor said, standing outside the patio with Sander, holding his hat in his hands. "But I would love to know I have your blessing. It is my intention to spend all my days and resources to make your daughter happy."

Sander clasped his hands behind his back. "I appreciate your coming to talk with me, man to man. You've made my daughter the happiest I've seen and also the most miserable."

He lowered his eyes. "I plan to give her nothing but good days going forward." When he heard a chuckle, his head snapped up.

"I'm just messing with you. From the moment I met those children of yours and watched Kelsey with them, I knew she was a goner. And I couldn't be more pleased as her father to know she'll be in good hands. And when the time comes, I'll proudly walk her down the aisle."

"I can say the same for me, sir. Thank you for raising such a wonderful daughter." His voice cracked. "She makes me the happiest man on the planet, and even more important, my kids absolutely adore her. I promise to be the man she deserves."

"That's all I need to hear, son." Sander got choked up too. "I've made many mistakes, but with Kelsey, I know I got that right. Take care of my baby girl."

* * *

Kelsey didn't sleep well last night. On the one hand, she wanted to do what was best for the children, but on the other, she loved spending time at her ranch. She had toggled between both possibilities until her head hurt.

Yet when she broached Trevor about it, he had left the decision solely up to her, which was why she was now sitting in Nancy's office.

"I'm torn," she said after filling her forewoman in on her dilemma. She massaged a knot in her neck.

"I think you're making this a bigger deal than it has to be." Nancy said. Her calm, assured tone made Kelsey lean forward.

"What do you mean?"

"You don't have to live here to be involved in the ranch. You've already proven that. Even though you've been living at the main house, you have been here for every major event—the starter herd arrival, the lambing—you haven't missed a thing."

"You're right. I haven't. Trevor's property is only few miles away and it would probably take twenty minutes tops to get here." Her chest loosened. "I'm thinking about this way too hard." She pointed at Nancy. "Plus I have the best forewoman running things."

Nancy cracked up. "I agree. And we have hired a good team of people, so you know that we've got things covered here in your absence, while you focus on building your new life with Trevor and the kids."

Kelsey relaxed against the chair. "Nancy, you are so right. I wish I had come to you sooner."

"I only pointed out the obvious," the other woman

said. "Now that that's settled, let's talk about your breeding plans for your starter herd."

As soon as their meeting concluded, Kelsey called Trevor and shared her decision. "I'm ready to move into our home."

He gave a big whoop. "Consider it handled."

Trevor paid the movers a hefty sum to get Kelsey moved out of the main house and into *their* home by the next evening. She had some childhood relics that she would have to sort through, but for the most part, she was all settled in. Now, Kelsey was downstairs puttering about in the kitchen with Amy. Though he had meant what he'd said when he'd asked where Kelsey wanted to live, Trevor was glad she had chosen here. Because there was now zero chance of another encounter with her father like the one that they'd had in the kitchen.

Thanksgiving was now only three days away, and they had three places to attend. Something Kelsey didn't know yet. But fortunately, he had the best solution.

If she agreed.

He peeked inside the blue bag. Hopefully, with a lot of help from a fine jewelry store in Dallas, he would be able to convince her. Gathering his courage, he headed down the stairs.

"Hey, what you have you been up to?" Kelsey asked, giving him a smile that brightened his heart. They decided to sleep in separate rooms since their engagement, which had been a sweet kind of torture.

"Just getting some stuff together. Amy went to take the triplets for a stroll in their stroller."

Kelsey was cutting up apples, and that chef's knife looked sharp, but she was moving like a pro. She had said something about making a pie or a tart, exactly what, he couldn't recall, but there were ingredients like vanilla, cinnamon and a pastry shell spread across the counter. One thing was certain, whatever it was, it was going to be good.

He wrinkled his nose and pointed. "Something is missing."

"What? What's missing?" Kelsey put down the knife carefully on the chopping board and washed her hands. She started tapping and lifting the ingredients to read them.

Biting back a smile, Trevor beckoned to her and went to sit on the couch. He could hear her fussing and muttering to herself about what she could have possibly forgotten. Then she came to sit next to him. "What is missing?"

Trevor lifted her chin with his index finger and gave her a tender kiss. Then he reached into the bag and took out the first of the four velvet boxes. Opening the box, Trevor presented it to her. "This is what's missing."

"You were messing with me?" Kelsey gave him a light jab. Then her eyes went round. "Hang on. You got me a ring?"

Patting the bag, he said, "I got several, but I'll explain in a minute." He got onto one knee as he had done when he proposed the first time.

She leaned back. "What are you doing? Um, you already asked, and I accepted. My answer isn't going to change."

Trevor chuckled. "Sweetheart, I love you." He placed

a hand over her lips. "Some things are worth a do-over." He took out the two-carat yellow diamond halo engagement ring set in platinum and placed it at the edge of her finger. "Kelsey, you've already made me the happiest man when you accepted my proposal." He moved it halfway up her finger. "If I searched high and low, I don't know if I could find a diamond with the brilliance that matches the sparkle in your eyes. But I hope this comes close." He moved it all the way and then kissed her finger.

"Whew. You have a way with words."

"It's you, Kelsey. You're the one inspiring all of this from me."

She inhaled and spread her fingers. "Oh, Trevor, it's stunning."

He returned to sit next to her, facing her so their knees touched. Then he took out the next two boxes. She gasped when she saw they were his and hers gold-crusted platinum wedding bands. "Kelsey, if it's alright with you, I'd love to marry you this spring."

Her mouth dropped. "But that's in *six months*!"

"It can be done."

She jumped to her feet and paced the room. "I don't know if that's doable. I really don't. People book their venues and all that a year or two in advance most of the time."

"Together, we have a large family, and we have resources."

He rested the bands on the coffee table then went over to where Kelsey stood and drew her to him. "I don't want a long engagement to make you my wife. I don't even want to wait another day." Then he gave her a searing and, he hoped, convincing kiss.

She looked at him, pools of desire in the green depths of her eyes. "What the heck... Let's do it!" She snapped her fingers. "Oh, and I just had a great idea."

"Do tell." He grinned.

"Well... I just remembered I already hired the caterer for our family Thanksgiving dinner. We can have an engagement party and tell everyone our good news then."

"Sheer genius." Steps light, Trevor went over to the couch and took out the final box. He gave it to Kelsey to open. She sucked in a breath and pulled out a bird-shaped brooch made of diamonds and platinum. The bird was already set on a blue emerald-cut stone.

"Aww. This is exquisite. How many times do you plan on making me cry today?" she sniffled.

Quirking his lips, Trevor texted Amy. *You can bring them in now.* A few minutes later, the sitter walked inside with his babies. Amy gave him a thumbs-up and hung back to watch. The triplets toddled toward Trevor and Kelsey, wearing mini Stetsons and matching green T-shirts.

He waited for Kelsey to read the white inscription on each of their tees. *Will You Be My Mommy?* She sobbed and nodded. "Yes, yes, yes. I'd like that very much." Then she gave each of them a kiss. "I can't wait to be your mom."

Chapter Seventeen

Pulling an engagement party together in a few days while running a ranch was up there on things she never imagined she would be doing.

But for Trevor...she'd move mountains.

Now, just because this was last minute and on a major national holiday, it didn't mean it had to *look* last minute. For Kelsey was a Fortune and Fortunes made things happen. And, as it happened, so did Porters.

Thanks to Hammond, who "knew a man," the cake, flowers and photographer were on lock.

Because of a last-minute cancellation, Kelsey had managed to secure the venue at the banquet hall at the Emerald Ridge Hotel, where she was able to use their caterers. This would give their family and friends a great reason to get dressed up and celebrate before the official holiday shopping season began. Priscilla and Zara were handling the decorations.

The only thing left was for her to choose what she would wear. The only thing she knew for sure was that she wanted an emerald-colored cocktail dress. Knowing her mother wasn't here to help with any of this or plan her upcoming wedding made her chest hurt.

But she had Priscilla and Zara and they would be heading over to the dress boutique that very afternoon.

Three hours and countless dresses later, Kelsey was still searching the rack when Trevor called. "Sweetheart, I have the most ridiculous question to ask you. Feel free to say no. You don't have to say yes."

He sounded so hesitant. "Okay... What is it?"

"Pop just told me that he has my mother's wedding dress in one of those forever bridal storage boxes. I can't believe he held on to it. He just gave it to me for Sasha to wear one day. But when I saw it, it took my breath away. I know this doesn't make any sense, but I just feel like you would look amazing in it. That's if you'd want to borrow it."

"Um, I don't know. How do you know it will even fit?"

His voice lowered. "I know your body, sweetheart. It will fit."

"Dang it. Stop sounding all sexy in my ear." Kelsey eyed the numerous gowns slung over chairs and the harried saleswoman, stacking dresses over her arm. What could it hurt? "I'll try it on, but I won't make any promises."

"That's fair. I honestly expected you to turn me down flat." Trevor said. "But again, no pressure to wear it."

"Got it."

Calling to Priscilla and Zara, Kelsey ushered them out the door and into the truck. "Trevor wants me to try on his mother's dress. She eloped, so I don't have high expectations, but Trevor is sure it will be a perfect fit."

"Will he be insulted if you don't wear it?" Priscilla asked.

"No. He knows it's my choice."

The minute Kelsey donned the dress, which was couture and definitely *not* simple, she knew it was the one.

"Every angle I look at is divine," Zara breathed out.

"I agree. If I didn't know better, I would think it was made for you," Priscilla said.

The dress had a cinched period corset, a French lace mermaid skirt and a statuesque silhouette. But Kelsey adored the off-the-shoulder gigot sleeves and the handmaid floral appliqués.

Turned out that Samira was every bit the billionaire's daughter. Even though she had eloped, she had purchased a luxurious gown. The thought of Trevor's mother wearing this gown in a courthouse was ridiculous and marvelous at the same time. A sign of a woman who had a mind of her own. And the most exquisite taste.

This engagement party was coming together the way it should.

Her life had changed. Permanently. The past few days had been such a whirlwind of activity that that fact hadn't hit Kelsey until just now. She stood in the center of what was now her former suite at the main house as she processed that she had truly flown the nest after twenty-five years.

She had so many memories here, so many milestones.

Leaving had been bittersweet, but Kelsey wanted to be sure her father would be okay.

She traipsed downstairs and into the kitchen. They were going to make s'mores and watch old family movies. It was one of their favorite things to do, and she was feeling especially nostalgic tonight.

"I've already laid everything out," Dad said, pointing to the graham crackers, milk chocolate and marshmallows.

"Yum. Do you have the ground cinnamon and cayenne?"

"Yep. There's also vanilla, almond extract and, of course, ground pecans."

Perfect. Sometimes, they liked to experiment to add flavor or spice, but for the most part, the traditional recipe was the way to go.

"Go ahead and make your own and we'll just pop them into the microwave," Dad said, tossing a marshmallow in his mouth.

Kelsey washed her hands and then stacked her s'more. "We should probably use the air fryer instead."

"Good idea." Her father went to crank it up.

Behind her, the television was already on and there was a video on pause. Her eyes strayed to the empty corner where the playpen had sat for weeks until Trevor left. Without the children about, the place had been restored to its original state.

The house now seemed stark.

Lonely.

"Dad, are you going to be okay with me gone?" Kelsey asked, going over to stand next to him.

"I'm thrilled to finally have the space all to myself." He bit into the s'mores. Some of the marshmallows ended up on his cheek.

"Stop deflecting, please. I need to know you're going to be alright." She wiped the side of his face.

"Listen, I'm too happy for you not to be. It was just us here for quite a few years, so I know that's going to take some getting used to, but I know you're with a man who's going to treat you right."

She placed her two sides for her s'more in the air fryer and lowered the temps. Kelsey wasn't sure how long it would need so she'd keep an eye on it.

"Yes, Trevor is wonderful, but you were the gold standard. I wouldn't have known what a good man should look like if it weren't for how you treated me, how you treasured me and, yes, how you spoiled me. If a man didn't measure up to you, they got the boot fast." She made a motion of kicking her heel.

"Aww, thank you. I was so young when I had you, I didn't know what I was doing. All I did was love you the only way I knew how." He gave her a tender look. "My baby girl is all grown up. I'm proud of the adult you've become, and your cousins."

"Thank you, Dad. We all turned out okay because of you."

Her dad tipped his Stetson. "If you don't stop lavishing me with praise, you're going to get me mushier than these marshmallows, and we can't have that."

"Only speaking the truth. I hope you'll open your heart to love again because you have so much to give. Plus, you're young. You shouldn't be alone."

"Is that why you keep enrolling me into all these activities, like pickleball? I'm good with my own company and I laugh at my own jokes. I know you're in love and you want everybody else to feel what you're feeling. But I promise you, it's all good here."

"Alright, Dad. I'll let it be." *For now.* Her s'more

looked ready, so she turned off the power. Her father had already nuked his second one.

They settled next to each other on one of the couches in the family area. "Now press Play. This is the one where Zara and Priscilla were chasing you around the boathouse to get you to learn how to swim." He cackled because he knew how much she hated that video.

"Dad, *really*? My cousins were so mean to me back then. Roth tossed me in the water, and you did nothing but laugh. I could've been eaten by a shark."

Suddenly, her father grew serious. "You really think I would have let you get in that water if there were predators about?" He gave a knowing look, one that said he was talking about swimming and more.

"No, Dad, you would not." She gave his hand a squeeze. "Thank you, Dad."

He touched her arm. "By the way, how are the wedding plans going?"

She expelled a breath. "One thing's for sure. I'm only doing this once. It been hectic, but I think it will all come together in the end."

"I know your wedding is months away but I have something for you." Wiping his hands on his apron, he hurried through the arched doorway into his private study. Kelsey followed behind.

When she was a child, Kelsey loved coming in here to snatch a book from the floor-to-ceiling oak bookcases. Her father would sit behind the drafting table, and she would either sprawl across the large leather sofa or in one of the cowhide chairs and read while he worked. Dad entertained most of his clients and contractors here since it had its own entrance and parking—that way they wouldn't walk through his home.

Her father went to his desk and puttered around until he picked up a black jewelry box and stretched it toward her. "Those were your mother's."

She peered at the little box, not daring to touch it. "You have something of my mother's?"

"Yes, I do. It was her grandmother's and something she valued as her single most prized possession. When Lani was pregnant with you, she said if anything happened to her, she wanted you to have them. Of course, neither of us imagined that she would be gone a month after giving birth to you. But I made sure to get these for you, and I restored them to mint condition."

Her eyes welled. "I can't believe you have this." Reverently, she took the small square out of his hand and opened it. What she saw made her gasp. "Pearl earrings." She traced the smooth tops of the round jewels. "They are lovely and sparkling," she whispered, picturing them dangling from her mother's ears.

"I had them professionally cleaned."

Her mother had touched these at one point in her life. And now Kelsey did as well. "Thanks so much, Dad. I'll treasure them," she choked out before hugging him. "You always know just what I need."

"Oh, honey..." He reached for a tissue and wiped her face. "It just fills me with such pride to think you'll have your mom with you on all your special days."

Looping her arm through his, she said, "I'll have both of you."

Epilogue

Six months later

It took intense concentration, since Trevor was kissing her neck...her earlobe...the space between her neck... But Kelsey managed to unlock the front door to their home with one arm draped around Trevor's shoulders.

"Are you sure no one will miss us?" After the ceremony, she had changed into a jumpsuit and bejeweled white sneakers while the rest of her bridal party had worn green jumpsuits. Trevor and his groomsmen had all changed into blue jeans, crisp white shirts, brown boots and white Stetsons. Then they had partied like nobody's business.

"Sweetheart, they would be surprised if we stuck around." Trevor cradled her against his chest and stepped over the threshold. He didn't put her down until they were in their bedroom. Neither had wanted to go on a honeymoon or leave the children for a prolonged period of time, but they knew they didn't want to share each other with anyone. They wanted to be in a bubble that night.

They wanted to be together in their home their first night as man and wife.

Suddenly, Kelsey felt shy, which was not like her. She

was about to make love to her husband for the first time as Mrs. Porter. Kelsey felt pressured to give him the most memorable night of his life. What if she didn't meet his expectations? Shoot, what if he didn't meet hers?

She lowered her lashes. "I'll be right back. I need to freshen up." And to think.

When Kelsey entered the bathroom, she gasped. There were candles lining the tub and rose petals in a warm bath. The scent of lavender filled the air, and a fruit and cheese tray were on a small table. How romantic. She stuck a finger in the water. It was really warm. She couldn't wait to get under that. Trevor came up behind her and wrapped his arms around her waist.

"When did you do this?" she asked, munching on a crunchy grape.

"I had some help." He raked his teeth across her earlobe, making her moan. Then Trevor unzipped her jumpsuit. Kelsey stepped out of it, and he sucked in a breath at her barely there lingerie. Whistling, his voice dripped with desire. "You didn't tell me all that was under there."

Turning around, she gave him a naughty grin before helping him out of his clothes. She had never seen a man get undressed so fast. That boosted her ego, knowing she was wanted like that. Holding hands, they stepped into the bathtub. Trevor gritted his teeth and stepped back. "Whoa, this is hot."

She chuckled, sinking under the water. "It feels glorious to me, and I love the scented oils."

It took a few seconds for Trevor to adjust to the temperature, then he put on some slow jams and drew her in for a kiss, his mouth hungry on hers. The water lapped about them as their passion grew. Her hands roamed his body, and her breath quickened. Kelsey wanted to stay here forever but goose bumps popped up on her skin. Seeing her shiver, Trevor pulled away. "Ready to get out?"

Kelsey nodded. After a quick rinse in the shower, Trevor and Kelsey wore matching his and her fluffy robes. Her stomach rumbled.

"Are you hungry?" Trevor asked.

"I guess the fruit and cheese weren't enough. I haven't eaten much all day, and I had only a small bite of our meal." The menu had been salmon on a bed of seasoned rice with grilled asparagus, and the little that she'd eaten had been delicious, but there were people to greet and guests to entertain.

"How about we head downstairs and get another snack?"

"I'd like that." Reaching out, he caressed her ear and then ran his hand through her curls before clearing his throat. "You were such a beautiful bride. I was awestruck watching you walk down the aisle. The closer you got to me, all I could think was, how did I get so lucky?"

"I was thinking the same when I saw you under the awning, each of your groomsmen holding one of the triplets. My heart was just so full." She molded her body to his. "I love you, Mr. Porter, and I don't want to sleep or catch a movie." Touching his face, she said, "I want to make love to my husband."

"And I love you, Mrs. Porter. With all my heart." He squared his shoulders. "Now, if you don't mind, I have an odd request."

"What's that?"

He held out a hand. Their wedding bands sparkled under the lights. "Join me in the kitchen."

"Alright..." Kelsey followed Trevor down the stairs. All the lights were off inside the house. Guiding her in the dark, Trevor turned on the light. Then he went to the refrigerator and took out a layer of their wedding cake, which he'd asked Kelsey's cousins to put in the fridge for them. Clearly having a big family paid off.

"Ooh, I'm so glad you saved that."

"I know traditionally, the top layer is saved for the anniversary, but I had something else in mind."

She arched a brow. "Oh?"

Trevor reached for a knife and cut a generous slice of vanilla cake with buttercream frosting, then placed it in front of her. She dipped her finger, took a small wedge and plopped it into her mouth. Closing her eyes for a second, she moaned. "This is delicious." When she opened her eyes, she sucked in a breath. The look in his eyes was almost...feral. She arched a brow. "You were saying?"

"I wanted a do-over," he growled. "Your father interrupted us, and I'd like to finish what we started that night. Do you remember?"

Did she remember? Her body burned at the memory. Kelsey had played back that scene too many times to count.

He grabbed her waist and grounded his hips into hers. Her robe fell open and so did his. She feasted her eyes on the evidence of his want for her, her mouth going dry. "I've been thinking about that night nonstop, and I wonder what would have happened if your father hadn't burst in on us."

Desire raged within her veins, and her pulse raced. "Let's see... Where were we?" Kelsey asked, throaty.

"I think I was here..."

A wicked glint in his eye, he pulled her down on the kitchen floor and proceeded to make love to her, adding fuel to the fire raging within. And this time there were absolutely no interruptions.

* * * * *

Look for the next installment of the new continuity
The Fortunes of Texas: Fortune's Hidden Treasures

Fortune's Unexpected Gift
by Jennifer Wilck.

On sale December 2025
wherever Harlequin books and ebooks are sold.

And catch up with the previous books:

His Family Fortune
by New York Times *bestselling author*
Elizabeth Bevarly

Fortune's Fake Marriage Plan
by USA TODAY *bestselling author*
Tara Taylor Quinn

Fortune for a Week
by USA TODAY *bestselling author*
Nancy Robards Thompson

Available now!